Fury of tl
The Sasquatch

By

Clint Romag

BOOKS BY CLINT ROMAG

CHRONICLES OF A WEREWOLF
The Werewolf Manuscript
Search For The Werewolf
The Werewolf King
Revenge Of The Werewolves
Damnation Of The Werewolf

THE SASQUATCH ENCOUNTERS
The Unleashing
The Ape Cave Horror
Fury Of The Sasquatch
The Yeti Incident
The Bigfoot Experiment
War Of The Sasquatch
Rise Of The Cryptids

LEGACY OF THE SASQUATCH ENCOUNTERS
The Bigfoot Contagion
The Bigfoot of the Deep
Flight of the Sasquatch

SHORT STORY COLLECTIONS
Titanius Seven
The Sasquatch Encounters SHORTS: The Complete Collection
Ressurection of the Werewolf

A Spreading Madness

For my niece Lilyauna Jude, who was born March 10, 2008, about the same time I started writing this book.

ACKNOWLEDGEMENTS

First, I would like to thank Andres Grau for the awesome new cover.

A big thank you for my Mom who continues to edit my books even though she wishes all the Sasquatch were dead. Thanks Mom!!!!!!!!!!!!!

A thank you for Virginia Franken and her English Proofing abilities for doing a final proofread.

NEW AUTHOR'S NOTE

I was excited to write this book because at the end of The Unleashing the Bigfoot disappear and I wanted to know where did they go next and what happpened to them. The Ape Cave Horror dealt with another group of Bigfoot so with this third book it ties closely with the first one.

I don't remember how I decided on the town of Hyder, maybe just looking at a map. I wanted to have the story take place in a small Alaskan town and I thought Hyder was in a perfect location near the southern border of the state.

Fury of the Sasquatch is the third part of the first trilogy in the series tying up many of the story lines and loose ends. It also opens up some new storylines and ideas that were hinted at in the earlier books which the next trilogy in the series goes into more depth starting with The Yeti Incident.

My friend told me recently that years ago he rented a car in Michigan and drove to Alaska and back. I would love to do the same from Washington State and drive to Hyder, Alaska. Maybe I would see some Bigfoot on the way.

Well, it's about to get tense, so it might be a good idea to lock your doors and windows while reading this book. Also, reading during daylight hours is preferred. The Bigfoot are about to be unleashed again!

Good luck!

Hope you enjoy!

Clint Romag
February 12, 2017

ORIGNAL AUTHOR'S NOTE

The Bigfoot Body was a hoax. I was so disappointed. When I first heard that two Pennsylvania men had found the corpse of an actual Sasquatch and were preparing to reveal thei findings, I was so excited. I was thinking how could it not be real if they had a body.

The story quickly made the national news and excitement was building. And then they showed a picture of the body in the ice chest. I immediately thought it looked like a costume and was disappointed. They were planning to have a news conference that Friday to reveal more evidence so part of me kept my hopes up and to reserve judgment until the conference.

And then the conference came and all they showed were a couple blurry photos and not much else and then I realized it was over. The body was a fake. If they really had the body they would have tons of detailed photos and would let the press see it.

The only good thing that came out of it was that Bigfoot was one of the top news stories across the nation for about a week.

So let's get on with the story.

Clint Romag
January 31, 2009

CHAPTER 1

A light snow floated lazily down, covering the forest floor and adding to the inches that had already accumulated on the ground from weeks of winter weather. It was near dusk but the white clouds above and the blanket of snow below reflected the failing light, making it much brighter than an ordinary snowless night. The air was crisp and cold and the woods, a couple miles outside of the small town of Hyder, Alaska, had an ominous quiet settle upon them as if in warning of the maelstrom to come. Clumps of snow fell from branches making an occasional smacking sound, but all the birds and animals seemed to have fled that particular area of the woods. There were no deer, squirrels, birds, or hares only a foreboding, eerie silence.

A different sound other than that of falling snow, broke the stillness, quiet at first but growing steadily louder. Forceful footsteps crunched through the snow at a steady pace as something of great weight was on the move. A hush settled upon the woods as if death itself approached. The crunching grew nearer and stopped as a massive, shadowy figure emerged from the undergrowth and halted near the gnarled trunk of a fir tree. The Sasquatch breathed in heavy and deep, steam blowing from its thick nostrils, as it stood motionless, blending in with the undergrowth. Its fierce, black eyes scanned the area ahead taking in every detail. A dusting of snow dotted the shaggy brown hair that covered its entire muscular body. Patiently it stood in one spot for several minutes, in no hurry to proceed until it was ready. Caution and stealth were always at the forefront of its thoughts and would hide as long as necessary.

A dog barked followed by the voices of at least two manthings somewhere up ahead beyond the line of trees, breaking the calm of the forest. The Sasquatch's eyes grew wide with brief surprise before a malicious scowl settled on its face. Its black claws dug into the bark of the tree it was standing near in anticipation as a growing fury became evident on its hairy, beastly face. Its eyes narrowed in deadly concentration, chomping its teeth, readying for war. It hated the manthings more than anything

The Sasquatch was a scout, the first to venture this close to the manthings' dwelling, which was filled with lights even at night, something it did not understand. It prided itself in this honor and it would not fail. The Scout listened to the approaching manthings and dog, so loud, so unaware that they were getting nearer to death. The Scout's stomach churned in hunger and its mouth watered at the thought of fresh meat. Its people had gone with little food for many months, scavenging for the few scraps they could find, a deer, fish, and an occasional bear. The Scout was always hungry and it wanted to eat and be full. The Scout breathed the fresh air; glad to be outside, tired of hiding in caves and darkness.

They had hidden far too long from these weak things that were more numerous than maggots and flies on a rotten corpse. The manthings had been hunting them relentlessly for years now after its people had attacked their camp and killed all of them, but one. A young male had escaped in one of their metal flying birds. It hated the fact that one of them had escaped. The Scout had tracked the young manthing to a lake. They had been so close to killing him. What could almost be described as a smile touched the Scout's hairy face as the thought of killing so many of the manthings crossed its mind. The Scout had gone with its brothers and had helped them slaughter every single one of them, except for the one that flew away.

Killing so many of them was something its people had dreamed of for as long as the Scout could remember. The elders had told stories of the hated manthings for generations. Manthings were weak, but there were so many of them, like ants, always spreading out, cutting down trees, building their dwellings of wood and rock that grew bigger and bigger. They were everywhere, taking more land, going into the woods over stone trails, zooming in their metal boxes and were even able to fly in the sky.

The Scout's people had always been on the run, moving deeper into the forests to higher ground and deeper caves, but the manthings always intruded into their territory. They had been running ever since the slaughter at the camp. Manthings had sent their metal flying birds after them, but its people were smart. The manthings had never found them. They had managed to avoid detection since that joyous day of destruction.

A rustle in the undergrowth signaled the arrival of the Scout's enemies as a dog, a black lab, bounded into view growling and sniffing. The Scout tensed, remaining still as the dog barked in

10

its direction. A manthing called out from behind the dog in the distance. The dog growled, lowering its head and moved slowly towards the tree. Without warning, hairy hands snatched the dog and pulled it behind the tree in one quick blur of motion. The Scout snapped the dog's neck and threw the animal back into the open. It moved behind the tree as the loud footsteps and calls from the manthing grew nearer.

"Trixsy, Trixsy… get back here," Chuck yelled pushing through the undergrowth into a small clearing where the broken body of his dog lay lifeless in the snow. "What the hell," he said in utter shock and rushed over to his dog. He kneeled down and examined the dog for moment before he glanced about in alarm, his face creasing with fear. He raised his hunting rifle and gasped when he saw the tall, dark shape of a man-like creature standing in the shadows of the undergrowth only twenty feet away staring at him with cruel, black eyes.

With only a brief hesitation, Chuck aimed his rifle and shot, but the shadowy figure had already moved behind the tree. "Bigfoot," he whispered in a panic. There had been Bigfoot sightings for the last six months in this area, enough so, that the famous Andrew Bridgeton and Chad Gamin had been staying in town for the last few weeks searching the area. It had been exciting to have two celebrities visit their small community and the entire town was buzzing with all of the attention. He and his buddy Spence had decided to go into the woods to capture one, a sure way to fame and wealth. He could hear his friend Spence call out his name from somewhere behind him in the undergrowth.

The Sasquatch roared, sounding deep, powerful and so monstrous that Chuck visibly shook and nearly dropped his rifle in fright. He had never heard anything so horrifying. It took several seconds to break free of the frozen shock that had descended over his body and force back the panic. Terrified, he fired his rifle at the foliage as he gritted his teeth and scanned the perimeter. The tree began to shake violently back and forth, creaking and cracking until the whole trunk fell towards him with a loud snap of wood. Chuck ran, trying to dodge it but slipped in the snow, falling on his face.

The Sasquatch charged forward, a massive dark shape bursting through the undergrowth, closing the distance between them with quick, long strides. Chuck gasped as the nightmarish beast, all hair, muscles and fierce black eyes, reached for him with a massive clawed hand. The Scout tore into Chuck with eager vengeance, slicing and stabbing as it growled and chomped its teeth. The manthing screamed and then went still as blood squirted and stained the snow red. The Scout stood up, its hair spotted with blood, snow and pieces of flesh.

Gunfire boomed behind the Scout as another manthing pressed through the undergrowth towards the clearing with a rifle in his hands. The Scout knew the rifle was dangerous even from a distance so it leaped over the fallen tree and lay flat on its stomach when the rifle thundered for a second time. It growled angrily and slid closer to the trunk of the fallen tree.

Spence moved into the clearing, his face white and lined with terror and confusion, wondering what the hell had happened. He had heard Chuck scream and then something roar which sounded as powerful and deafening as a lion's roar. He then saw a tree crash down. "What the hell is going on?" he thought as he moved into the clearing and caught a glimpse of a giant beast leap over the fallen tree and duck down. Spence fired his rifle, the sound thundering through the woods. Whatever was on the other side of the tree began to growl, deep and angry.

Spence moved further into clearing, each step crunching loudly in the snow. "Get out of here," Spence yelled and moved towards his friend, who lay motionless in the blood splattered snow. "Leave us the hell alone," he yelled with desperation and fired again, unable to see the beast hidden beyond the branches of the tree trunk. He heard it growl and breathe, deep and heavy.

Spence glanced down at his friend and grimaced at the sight of the mutilated body, which had been hacked and slashed. It had broken Chuck's neck and his skull was bashed. Spence backed away several steps and spotted Chuck's dog in a pool of blood. He began to hyperventilate as his stomach churned in disgust. His hands were trembling as the beast began growling louder.

The thought that he was now alone in the woods, next to his friend's dead body, twisted out of control making his panic explode. Why had they been so stupid? This beast had to be a Bigfoot. There had been Bigfoot sightings for months and Bigfoot hunters had come to town warning everyone to be careful. Why had he not listened to them? They had lived in Hyder all of their lives and had hunted these very woods ever since they were in middle school. They knew the area well and could not pass up a chance to capture one of these fabled animals dead or alive. They had never once been scared. They men and women attacked at Mount Saint Helens had been pussies and cowards. Spence and his friends were great marksmen and had never been scared hunting deer, elk or bear, but this was entirely something beyond his worst nightmare. Now that he had gotten a glimpse of the monster, he was ready to crap his pants. All the bravado and confidence he had displayed a few minutes ago was now gone.

"I have to stay calm," he thought backing away from the fallen tree as the growling continued in menacing tones. He glanced frantically about wondering if there were more than one of them. What if he was surrounded? He had to return to the truck and get the hell out of the woods.

The fallen tree started to shake, its branches creaking and needles falling as the Bigfoot roared, the sound echoing through the forest. Spence froze at the ferocity of the noise and then slipped, falling down into the snow. The tree continued to shake as it was raised up and thrown. The trunk slammed a few feet in front of him, some of the branches scraping his face. Spence yelled, grabbed his rifle and staggered to his feet gasping in terror. He turned and fled back the way he had come, out of the clearing and into the undergrowth.

The Scout growled louder in anticipation of the hunt. The manthing was weak and had already started to flee like some puny little animal thinking he could escape. The manthing had no chance. The Scout climbed over the branches eager to end his pathetic, little life.

The Scout tasted some of the blood on its fingers, savoring the salty flavor, before leaping over the tree and smacking loudly in the snow on the other side. With its black claws outstretched, the Scout pursued its prey.

CHAPTER 2

"My ex-wife is a bitch," Andrew Bridgeton suddenly said in a burst of anger. His gray eyes were livid as his wrinkled face creased deeply. The white bangs of his hair fell down on the front of his forehead; he brushed them aside in annoyance. He sat alone at a small neighborhood bar on the outskirts of Hyder, Alaska. The few patrons looked up at him in amused surprise.

"Mine too," a burly man with a cigar called out and everyone laughed.

Andrew finished his martini and ordered another. "Lots of olives this time."

"I haven't made this many martinis in years," the bartender said with a hearty laugh. "You've ordered more maritinis than the entire town has in the last five years. Most people around here drink beer and shots of the hard stuff."

Andrew nodded in a curt manner, his thoughts elsewhere. He had been coming to this bar, Trapper's Delight, opened in 1925, for the last three weeks, since he had arrived in town. It was his refuge from the cold days out in the wilderness and a diversion from his dark thoughts and emotions. The bar was old with mahogany tables and chairs that were stained with years of cigarette and cigar smoke, and spilled beer. It was a real bar with a warm, cramped atmosphere, where people still smoked, unlike the sterile, lifeless bars he was use to in the lower 48 states.

The bartender, a man in his mid-sixties, around Andrew's age with a thick white beard and a bald head, began making the martini. "Any Bigfoot news?" The bartender asked in a throaty, gruff voice.

"Sasquatch," Andrew snapped and shook his head, plopping an olive in his mouth. "Not today, but we will find them, I promise you that."

"It just might put this damn city on the map," The bartender mused as he brought him the drink.

"Indeed." Andrew's thoughts returned to his ex-wife. It had been over a year since the "Ape Cave Horror," as the news had dubbed it, and she had been a thorn in his side ever since, blaming him for his beloved daughter's death. Andrew tightened his jaw at the thought of his daughter Sherrie; the image of her lying dead in the forest, murdered by one of the Sasquatch, would never leave his mind. It had been too much holding his daughter's lifeless body waiting for the police to arrive. He had held her many times as a child, always laughing and asking questions and now she was dead, killed by the animals he had spent his life searching for.

"Oh Sherrie," he whispered taking a sip of his martini. His wife had tried suing him for wrongful death and reckless endangerment and everything else she could pull out of her ass. The lawsuit had painfully come to an end a month ago and he was finally vindicated, innocent, but it had taken time, so much of his time. He gritted his teeth at the thought. After 40 years of searching for the Sasquatch, he had actually found them and instead of spending all his energy on studying the captured corpses, writing books, giving speeches, he was fighting a damn lawsuit.

"At least it's over with," he mumbled. "Now I can get on with my real work."

The door opened and a blast of frigid air chilled the bar as Chad Gamin walked in bundled in a heavy jacket and wearing a blue hat pulled all the way down to his eyebrows. In his early thirties, his face was red and unshaven. He sat on the bar stool next to Andrew, ordered a beer and said, "Damn it's cold."

"Find anything in the south hills?" Andrew asked, his face growing stern.

Chad shook his head. "No… nothing. Alberto and I spent the entire day hiking around checking the cameras we set in the area two weeks ago. The only pictures were of deer and a couple bears."

"Spot any caves? There are obviously some caves in the area that we don't know about. That's where our elusive prey have been hiding. I guarantee you." Andrew chewed on another olive from his martini and frowned, frustrated. "If they were out in the open we would have detected them with the infrared cameras in the helicopter by now. They are in the earth, hiding away in the dark."

"Maybe this is a wild goose chase," Chad said. "Maybe they're not up here. We've been searching for three weeks and nothing."

"The group of Sasquatch from Canada, who attacked Camp Elizabeth, are up here, "Andrew mused. "I can feel it, just like I did at Mount Saint Helens. I feel it deep in my bones."

A shiver went down Chad's spine as he thought of the Sasquatch he had faced at Camp Elizabeth. They had killed his father, his childhood friend Shane, Meredith, Jay and many others. He forced back the sudden fear he felt and the unwanted memories and took a drink of his beer. He had faced these monsters twice, once in Canada and once at Mount Saint Helens and he was tired of being scared, one reason why he had joined up with Andrew. He wanted to face his fears and get revenge for his father's death. "Maybe it's some random Sasquatch and not the horde that I faced," Chad offered up.

Andrew shook his head sternly. "No, it's them. It's been four years since they attacked Camp Elizabeth, killing thirty people and then disappearing without a trace as if they had never existed. We know one fact; they left that area immediately after the attack. The police, hunters, rescue crews and reporters swarmed that entire forest and all they found was an empty cave containing a few dead bodies of some of their victims.

"As you know, I've shown you the charts of the data I've been collecting. I've been keeping track of any Sasquatch sightings or anything out of the ordinary several hundred miles in all directions from the epicenter, which is Camp Elizabeth. I'm keeping a record of everything, whether a hiker disappears, there's a drop in the deer population, reports of strange sounds or whatever. We know they are on the move, but where are they going? All the data points lead to this town. Over the last four years they've been migrating west and then there were several sightings the last six months in this area. They have stopped at this location. I don't know why, but I will find them. This is the jackpot."

"Or hell on earth." Chad laughed and took another swig of his beer.

"Where is Alberto by the way?" Andrew asked. Alberto was the brother to Enrique and nephew to Javier, both of whom were killed during the "Ape Cave Horror." Andrew promised to help out their family and hired Alberto to join the team during the last year.

"He went to the inn and said he was going to take a long, hot shower. Being from Florida, he's never experienced such cold weather." Chad finished his beer. "I think I'm going to do the same. I'm freezing, tired and dirty."

The door opened sending in another blast of cold air. Stephen Denmin, who was funding the operation and whose wife Claire was also killed by a Sasquatch, walked in with his men. "Andrew, Chad," Stephen greeted in his loud voice. "Any luck today?"

Both of them shook their head.

"We found a few footprints, but they were old, may have been made by human or bear. Just keep up the hard work. We'll find these bastards," Stephen said and ordered a drink.

Despite being overbearing and demanding at times, Chad would always feel indebted to Stephen for saving his life. It was Stephen who had flown a plane to the lake where Chad, the only one left alive, had taken a boat into the water hoping to escape the monsters. He found out that the Sasquatch could swim when they came after him like sharks. Stephen had flown him out of the area and found out at the same time the sad fact that his wife had been killed and his cabin burned down. Stephen had also been paying Chad for his expertise for the last couple years. Stephen had dedicated his life to finding and eradicating the Sasquatch who had killed his wife. He was just as obsessed as Andrew about finding these creatures. Chad ordered another beer as Stephen took a shot of tequila.

"Oh," Stephen coughed and cleared his throat. "You're not going to believe this Andrew. Reports just came in about a Yeti sighting in the Olympic mountain range. A hiker got a blurry picture of this white hairy shape."

"A Yeti in Washington State," Andrew huffed. "Preposterous. The Yetis are in the Himalayans."

"That may be…it's probably a prank, but I'll have one of my men check it out. Want to join us for a steak?"

"I'm going back to the inn," Chad said.

"No thank you." Andrew shook his head.

"Okay boys, see you tomorrow." Stephen left the bar followed by his men, all except for one.

Victor Morey, a tall, skinny man with glasses, his black hair always combed back, walked over with a disapproving frown on his face. "Don't drink too much. We're not paying you to have a hangover. We want you fresh. We still have a lot of ground to cover."

"Go away," Andrew snapped, glaring at him.

A scowl settled on Victor's face and his eyes grew hard and cold before he turned and walked out of the bar.

"I don't like that man," Andrew shook his head. "I don't trust him."

"What's his deal?" Chad asked. "He's always been an ass to me."

"He's sees us as the outsiders, most likely jealous of us since we've seen the Sasquatch first hand. He was head of a biotech company that Stephen bought out two years ago. Since then, Victor quickly became Stephen's second in command. Stephen's only goal is the destruction of the Sasquatch and has been dismantling his mining company selling land, equipment, and mining rights to funnel millions into his one goal of eradicating the 'monsters' that killed his wife. Much of the money is going to some secret project, which Victor is heading. Stephen won't tell me about it, but his attitude has changed from killing all Sasquatch to possibly capturing them."

"Isn't that what you want?" Chad asked. "To capture them. There was a time when you thought that they were the most peaceful creatures on the planet, allowing no guns except for tranquilizer weapons on your expeditions."

Andrew shook his head. "I was a fool. Maybe Javier, Enrique and Sherrie would have…"

"You can't think like that," Chad cut in. "We all have regrets and hindsight always gives us a better view of what we should or should not have done. It's too easy to look back and say, why didn't I do this instead."

"You're right Chad. It's just… it's hard at times."

"I know I'm going through the same thing."

"I've spent 40 years of my life searching for these creatures and even after the Mount Saint Helens fiasco, I tried to keep my emotions detached so I could study them. We've learned so much in the last year from the skeletons we found and the body of the one I killed. These animals are not apes, not some missing link, not some type of primitive man, but an entirely new species, undiscovered until now. I've wanted to capture and study them all my life. We could learn so much more from a live specimen and so many questions could be answered. How intelligent are they? Do they have a language? Would we be able to communicate with them? I've told you many times how the Grandfather had tried communicating with me in the cave, making grunting and clicking sounds and hand gestures. Question after question could be answered, but then all my curiosity ends, replaced with a hot ire when I think of my daughter. They killed Sherrie and I can't stop thinking about it. I don't know how I'll react if I ever see one again."

"Part of me hopes we never will," Chad said.

Andrew nodded. "You're a good man Chad. I'm glad I met you."

"The feeling's mutual," Chad replied, surprised that Andrew was opening up. Usually, he kept his feelings inside. They talked for while longer and then Chad left the bar and started for the inn. Andrew sat at the bar alone, finishing his martini as his thoughts returned to his daughter.

CHAPTER 3

Spence charged through the undergrowth running for his life as the sounds of growling and heavy footsteps crunching in the snow behind him grew louder and closer with each passing second. He knew the lay of the land well, having hunted these woods since he was a young boy with his father. He bolted left towards the stream that chattered ahead of him, which was the fastest way to his truck. The sounds of pursuit seemed to get a little farther away. Maybe he would make it and escape from this nightmare. It was all happening too fast. His long time friend Chuck was dead. They had spent the day together telling stories of their high school days, joking around, drinking beer and eating lunch, and now he was dead. It was too much to even comprehend.

Spence jumped down the bank of a wide stream mostly covered in ice. The water churned underneath, moving along the rock bed. Spence slipped, fell to the ground and pulled himself up with the help of some roots that were sticking out from the wall of the bank. He moved as quickly as he could over the ice, which cracked with each slippery step.

Branches and leaves exploded outward to his right as the Sasquatch leaped from the shadows of the bank and landed twenty feet from him breaking the ice underneath its weight. Startled, Spence stepped back, his foot shooting through the ice. Luckily the water was only a couple feet deep. He scrambled out of the hole and crawled across the remainder of the ice until he had reached the far bank.

The Sasquatch stepped through the ice in a straight line towards him. Spence struggled up the slope and pushed through a tall bush surrounded by foliage that was still covered with leaves. He was almost to the truck. Fleeing away from the stream in a panic, he was vaguely aware that he still had the rifle gripped tightly in his hand. A loud crash and snapping branches warned that the Sasquatch had climbed up the bank close behind him.

With a renewed sense of desperation, Spence ran as fast as he could through the snow, branches whipping across his face, scraping him as he pushed through the heavy undergrowth. A fallen tree lay in front of him creating a four-foot tall barrier. Without slowing, he leaped and rolled over the top of the rotten tree.

It almost seemed unreal that a Sasquatch was chasing him. He had doubted the reports about old man Willard claiming to see a Bigfoot crossing his back yard late one night a few months back. After that first, initial sighting, people started to find Bigfoot prints in the area, but Spence thought it was due to everyone's over active imagination. The prints were most likely human or even old bear prints. He was sure that some practical jokesters could have created them. It had been the talk of the town for the last few months and it seemed to have gained some validation when the Bigfoot hunters arrived to investigate.

Spence had seen Andrew Bridgeton and Chad Gamin on television in the news reports, documentaries and interviews. It had been kind of cool to see them in person and he even said hello to them one night when they had been shopping in the general store. That is when Spence and his buddy Chuck had decided to go hunting for the creature themselves with thoughts of fame and wealth.

"And now Chuck's dead," Spence thought as he broke free from the thick undergrowth and headed into the clearing towards his parked truck. The Bigfoot growled behind him as it crashed through the bushes. Spence's jaw dropped, agape, suddenly remembering that the keys to his truck and his cell phone and been in Chuck's backpack.

"Damn it," Spence cursed between gasps of air. He continued running towards the truck desperately trying to decide what to do next. Branches cracked behind him and Spence glanced back to see a massive shape appear between the trees getting closer to the edge of the clearing. He rushed over to his truck, tired, and gasping. He doubted he could outrun the monster so he stopped abruptly in the middle of the clearing, in the failing light of dusk and raised his rifle to make his stand. His hands were cold and trembling, his face tight and focused as he faced the monster.

The Scout came to an abrupt halt as it approached the clearing finding that the manthing had stopped running and was pointing his weapon in its direction. The Scout knew the manthing's thunder stick could be deadly. Those booming sticks had killed several of its brothers during the attack at the camp long ago. It reached the edge of the clearing and ducked behind a tree. It roared and a loud explosion of gunfire boomed through the forest. The Scout tensed at the sound. It would not be discouraged. It picked up a heavy branch and hurled it into the clearing. This seemed to startle the manthing, who staggered back several feet and began to yell angrily. The Scout did not understand what its prey was saying, but it could detect fear in his voice. This show of weakness pleased the Scout.

The Scout dropped to the ground and began crawling to a different location. The manthing fired in its direction, but it kept moving, unafraid. It stood up behind another tree and grabbed the trunk with its powerful hands. It began to shake the base as the branches whipped back and forth. The manthing fired again and yelled.

Snarling its teeth, the Scout grew frustrated, deciding it was time. It raised its head up to the sky and shrieked, a shrill, punctuated screaming sound that caused the forest to go still. It continued to shake the tree making monstrous, screeching noises. The manthing fired again, but the Scout was undeterred and let loose a haunting wail. It stopped shaking the tree and waited, catching a glimpse through the foliage of the weakling prey standing in the middle of the clearing.

In the distance, a shrill scream rose in volume, followed by another and another in all directions. The Scout's black eyes brimmed with satisfaction as it roared, responding in answer to its brothers. The time of waiting and hiding like some helpless weak animal was over. The fury of the Sasquatch would be unfurled that night. They would be the aggressor and no longer would they hide meekly. The Scout looked at the manthing whose face was pale, white like the snow. The Scout could smell the fear. Its mouth watered, anxious to bite into the warm flesh. It was ravenous and wanted to feast.

"There's more," Spence whispered in panic still standing in the middle of the clearing as shrieking wails rose in the forest all around him. He had hoped that he was up against a lone Bigfoot, praying that it would take the bait and come into the clearing where he would have an open shot to kill it, but it had stayed hidden behind a tree. The monster was smarter than Spence had thought.

Shrill screeches continued to burst into the air as if a horde of demons had just been released from hell, a sound so terrifying that he nearly collapsed from fright. He felt weak in the knees and kept glancing about for a way to escape. There was no chance he could face several of these monsters and survive. "If only I had my damn keys," he thought and realized he had to act now.

Spence gasped and stumbled back a few steps as a tall, man-like shape appeared in the shadows of the tree line watching him with black eyes. Another giant figure stepped next to a tree, followed by another and another, until at least a dozen of these creatures stood at the edge of the clearing staring at him. Spence turned and sprinted down the road back towards town. The Carson's house was a short distance away and if he could make it there and call for help, he might have a slim hope of surviving. He knew Bob had several rifles. As he started to run, a sudden, hellish chorus of roars erupted through the forest. Loud crunching footsteps pounded the frozen ground as branches snapped behind him.

Spence did not dare look back as he ran as fast as could down the gravel road, which was covered in patches of frozen snow, his legs aching and his lungs burning. He navigated down the center avoiding some of the deep grooves from tire tracks. The sun had set and the sky was quickly growing darker.

The horde of Bigfoot pursued him with a relentless fervor, getting closer every moment; their loud steps thumped hard against the frozen ground and branches snapped and cracked as they charged through the undergrowth, spreading out to surround him. Spence could hear the beasts not only behind him but also to the left and right.

"They're trying to cut me off," Spence thought in horror as he rounded a bend in the road and to his relief, saw the Carson house with lights in the windows. Spence pushed himself to his limits, his muscles aching as he wheezed and gasped trying to catch his breath. He leaped a gully along the road and scrambled over a wooden fence. He ran across the pasture towards the house yelling, "Help me. Help."

The fence behind him shattered in a thunderous cracking sound as the Bigfoot broke through with apish shrieks. "Help," Spence yelled as he ran towards the porch. A dark silhouette appeared in the window looking out. Spence rushed forwards. "Mr. Carson. Help… it's me… Spence."

The door opened and Mr. Carson, a burly, gray-bearded man in his mid sixties, opened the door holding a rifle. He flipped on the porch lights and yelled, "Who the hell…" he stopped mid sentence, his eyes growing wide in shock as he saw several monstrous shapes rush through the pasture towards his home.

Spence barreled up the stairs. "They're after me. Get back into the house." Spence charged past Mr. Carson and pushed through the door into the living room where Mrs. Carson sat in front of the television with an alarmed look on her face.

Mr. Carson slammed the door and dead bolted it. "What the hell are those things?"

"Bigfoot," Spence gasped. "We have to call for help."

At that instant, the entire front window in the living room shattered, exploding inwards as a dark, hairy shape leaped through landing with a loud thump. The Sasquatch stood up to its full height of eight feet and roared as Mrs. Carson cried out and fell back against the couch, shuddering in terror. Somehow Spence managed to keep his wits and raised the rifle in his trembling hands, pointed the gun and fired, striking the beast in the chest. The Bigfoot stumbled back. Spence fired again and again until he was out of bullets. The monster collapsed on the floor knocking a chair and a bookcase over as it fell. A couple pictures on the wall dropped from the impact.

Two more of the monsters leaped through the window one after another. The first grabbed Mrs. Carson and pulled her up from the couch as the front door cracked and busted off of its hinges sending Mr. Carson sprawling to the floor, his rifle sliding out of reach. A Bigfoot entered, kneeled down and began strangling Mr. Carson with its huge, powerful hands. The Bigfoot that held the screaming Mrs. Carson flung her into the wall, bones cracking.

Spence dropped his empty rifle and fled down the hallway as more Sasquatch invaded the house, their monstrous shrieks blaring loudly. Spence reached the back door as Mr. Carson's yells were cut short. He opened the door and rushed down the steps praying that no Sasquatch were on this side of the house yet. He ran across the yard towards the road heading for town as the inhuman screams and shrieks echoed through the night sky.

CHAPTER 4

"And I thought Longview was small," Chad mumbled as he left the only bar in Hyder, Alaska. His hometown felt like New York compared to Hyder, which only had a population of 100. He had never heard of Hyder until a few months ago when there was a flurry of Bigfoot sightings and the discovery of some footprints. Andrew decided that this was it. This was where they would find the Sasquatch that had attacked Camp Elizabeth four years before. They had been here for three weeks and had found nothing yet, although Chad had been enjoying the trip. Surrounded by forest, mountains, lakes and rivers, Hyder was situated in the middle of majestic country.

Chad looked around and took a breath of the cold evening air. Hyder only had one main gravel road with a few side streets situated next to the Salmon River, which he could hear in the distance. He was staying with Andrew and Alberto at the south end of Hyder at an inn. Stephen and his group were residing in a motel in Stewart, B.C., two miles away across the Canadian border. Stewart was slightly bigger than Hyder with a population of 500 and had a few more roads, stores and restaurants. The two towns were in the middle of the wilderness, isolated from the rest of the world.

From the north end of town, Chad walked south towards the inn. A few people were outside walking and waved or said hello as they passed. An occasional car would drive by, rumbling over the gravel. He walked by a one-story log cabin with smoke billowing out of the chimney into the night sky. To his right on the other side of the Salmon River was a steep mountain of rock that rose into the sky, covering much of the horizon. Hyder was snuggled in a mountain valley. He had learned that Hyder was one of the few Alaskan towns that a person could drive to from the lower 48 states. Most towns could only be reached by plane or boat.

Chad passed several one-story houses with pointed roofs, many with porches. It was a quiet place, where time seemed to slow down. Nobody appeared to be in a hurry and Chad enjoyed it. He had lived in both ends of the spectrum: big city life in Los Angeles and the small town of Longview, Washington. A content, but tired expression settled on his face. "I think I've conquered my fear of the forest," he thought.

It had been over four years since the massacre at Camp Elizabeth, where he had witnessed the death of his father. The monsters murdered thirty people and sometimes it still seemed like it had only happened yesterday. The memories and nightmares were permanently seared in his mind and most likely would be for the rest of his life. During the three years following that awful trip, Chad had never ventured back into the woods, living briefly in Seattle and then moving back to Longview to be closer to his mom.

And when he finally did go back into the woods about a year ago, after Andrew had recruited him and Stephen had bullied him, he faced more Bigfoot at Mount Saint Helens in what became known as the "Ape Cave Horror." Most people would have never left the city after what he had experienced, but Chad had decided to face his fears, joining up with Andrew, in part because Sherrie, Andrew's daughter had been killed and Chad felt partially responsible. They had almost escaped when a giant Bigfoot had grabbed her from the hole they were hiding in. Chad always wondered if he could have done something different to save her life. He had an affinity to Andrew, both of them losing a family member to these beasts. So during this last year he faced his fears and had been tramping through the woods of the northwest in search of a monster that had caused so much destruction in his life. At first, Chad had to fight back panic attacks and sometimes he had to cut off the hikes early, imagining that a Bigfoot was behind every tree. It took a while for him to control his fears, taking comfort in the fact that the odds of ever running into one again were miniscule. He always traveled armed with at least a gun and of course Vengeance, his knife with a seven-inch blade, a square wooden handle, and a silver band along the edge with his initials etched in it. The anger that always burned in the back of his mind helped him keep his courage up; part of him wanted revenge.

Chad walked by the post office, a one story building with dark windows. The road he walked along had little light except for a couple streetlights that were too far apart. He reached the general store, a brown, two story building that looked like a big barn and decided to enter. They had a sub shop and he hoped it was still open. Chad walked up the wooden, creaking stairs and opened the front door, which had a bell on it that jingled. Part hardware store, part grocery store, part pawn shop, part tourist store, the place seemed to have everything one could imagine crammed in the narrow aisles.

"Chad," greeted Mrs. Measly from behind the cash register. She was an old, chubby woman with gray, curly hair with a big, friendly smile on her face. "How are you? Haven't seen you for a couple days."

"I've been hiking around the hills south of here." Chad walked over and could not help but smile back. Everyone in town seemed so friendly.

Mrs. Measly nodded, hey eyes brimming with excitement. "That's a beautiful area, a big tourist attraction during the summer. Lots of bears are in the river feeding on salmon. Not many bear are out at this time of the year… hibernation and everything. Did you see any Bald Eagles?"

"A couple," Chad said. "Is the sub shop still open?"

"It's closing soon, but if you hurry I'm sure you'll make it in time. We don't want you to go hungry searching for Bigfoot. A young man like yourself needs to eat. Mr. Measly, bless his heart, ate all the time. He worked on one of the fishing boats before he ran the store. He loved to barbecue. He was always eating."

Chad walked upstairs to the second level and to the back wall where Mrs. Measly's grandson sat behind the sub counter with a bored expression drawn over his face. He was a skinny high school kid with thick black hair combed forward like The Beatles during the early 1960s.

"Hi Chad," Eric said grinning, his eyes full of awe. "Can I have your autograph?"

Chad gasped, bewilderment lining his face. "My autograph?

"You're famous… I saw the movie about you… the Bigfoot movie about Camp Elizabeth. I heard they are making a sequel about your adventure at Mount Saint Helens."

"They may," Chad said, "but we're still in talks. It's a delicate matter since my friends died there."

"Geez, I never thought of it that way, but I still want your autograph." Eric handed him a napkin and a pen.

Chad signed the napkin with an amused smirk on his face as he ordered a sub. He sat down at one of the four tables and ate alone. At one time in his life, he had wanted to write screenplays. It was the reason why he had moved to Los Angeles to pursue his dream. He had only ended up getting bitter and frustrated before he went on vacation with his father to Camp Elizabeth. It seemed a lifetime ago when he had lived in Los Angeles, without a clue of the horror he would face. "Things were simpler," he thought. "My problems back then were nothing now that I think about it. Death puts things in perspective."

After the massacre at Camp Elizabeth, agents and movie producers tried to buy the rights to his story. He sold them, needing the money and a very cheesy, B-horror movie was made with awful special effects and pretty actors that could not act. And now it was happening again, but this time there were even more agents, producers and others trying to secure the rights to the "Ape Cave Horror." Chad was going to be careful this time out of respect to Andrew, whose daughter Sherrie and the rest of his team had been killed. The movie had to have at least some quality and be respectful to the people that were actually murdered. Whatever deal was made Andrew and Chad had agreed to split the money.

Chad ate his chicken sandwich, potato chips and finished his diet coke, feeling full and much better. His muscles were sore from hiking and climbing day after day. He was still amazed at how Andrew, who was 68, who had a bad knee and used a cane, was able to hike all day long, everyday. "I guess 40 years of Sasquatch hunting keeps you fit," he thought as he said goodbye to Eric and walked back down to the front of the store.

"How was dinner?" Mrs. Measly asked.

"Just as good as last time. Where's your candy?"

"Down the second aisle."

Chad started for the aisle and stopped abruptly throwing a troubled glance towards the front door. He listened for a few seconds, his face growing pale. "What was that?" Chad asked.

"What?" Mrs. Measly asked.

"I heard something scream outside." Chad rushed to the front door.

"My hearing is bad," Mrs. Measly said. "I'm almost seventy you know."

Chad opened the door and walked out onto the porch, his eyes wide with a deep fear. The town was quiet, still and dark. Chad's hand touched the hilt of Vengeance as he looked down the shadowy road toward the houses. Behind them was a black wall of trees where the forest started. He listened and glanced down the empty street. He noticed he was breathing faster and his chest was tense. He heard Mrs. Measly call from behind asking what he had heard. Chad continued to look around as a cold wind rustled through the branches of nearby trees. "It sounded like the roar of a Sasquatch," he whispered, feeling suddenly very alone.

CHAPTER 5

The Scout watched as its brothers stormed the manthing's house. There was a sound of gunfire and brief, desperate screams from the manthings. It flashed its teeth in satisfaction knowing that its enemies were dying. The Scout's eyes narrowed and looked to the left of the house, hearing the faint crunch of snow in the distance. It stood up from its hiding place in the pasture and moved quickly across the front yard with long strides, its feet making deep footprints. It rushed past the house and stopped near the back wall kneeling down, knowing full well that the manthing's fire weapons could strike from a long distance. Its black eyes caught movement and focused on the shadowy silhouette of a manthing climbing over a fence and running down the road.

The Scout stood up, its nostrils flaring as it sniffed picking up the scared scent of its prey. Anger rushed into its eyes as it realized that the manthing it had been chasing in the woods was the same one that was now escaping. It raised its head and made a high-pitched, shrill shriek, punctuated by three intense, sharp bursts of sound. In the distance short harsh shrieks replied from various directions. The Scout signaled the others and started to pursue the manthing. It charged across the yard, smashing through the wooden fence and ran down the road.

Spence fled in terror sprinting down the road as the ungodly cries came from all directions. How many damn monsters were there? It sounded like they were everywhere. The Carson's were dead in an instant and it was his fault. A pang of guilt filled his mind briefly for leading the monsters to them, but panic ravaged his mind and his only thought was survival, to reach town and find help. Breathing hard and quick, white in the face, Spence pushed himself to run faster, adrenaline pumping through his body. The fence behind him cracked loudly and he turned to see a giant Bigfoot break through and begin to pursue him.

Spence turned a corner in the road and on his right was the Smith's home. Seeing a light in the front window, he kept running for town passing by the house. He would not be safe in the house and did not want to bring death to the Smiths as well. The Carson's blood would be enough for him to deal with. He had known them all his life. Mr. Carson owned a boat and took tourists out fishing in the Portland Canal during the summers. Spence had worked for him a couple years during high school. Mrs. Carson would always cook wonderful, big meals, usually spaghetti, enough to last days. Now they were gone, killed by Bigfoot.

Everyone in town had been so excited about the Bigfoot sightings, the attention from the press, and the arrival of the Bigfoot hunters, but now the reality of what it actually meant stuck in his mind like a stake. Three people were already dead. How many more would die before this night was finished?

Hyder was a very small town and everyone knew each other, aware of all that was going on, hearing all the gossip. No one could hide secrets in such a small place. The entire town was like one big family, everyone helping each other out during hard times and now three of his friends were dead in one night.

Chuck, his best friend since childhood, was dead. Why had they gone into the woods in the first place? They had always gone hiking, hunting, and bear watching all their lives. How was this supposed to be any different? Spence did not want to think about breaking the news to Chuck's mom, a widow of four years.

Spence glanced back and saw the giant monster chasing him, closer than before and behind it were several others, some of them veering off to the Smith's house. Seconds later the sounds of glass shattering and wood cracking filled the air as the beasts attacked. The Smiths would not have a chance, caught by surprise by these murderous monsters. Part of him wanted to run back and try to help but there was nothing he could do without a weapon. He had to reach town, sound the alarm and get a gun. He hoped a car would drive by and pick him up. Maybe the lights of the car would scare the Bigfoot off? He doubted it since gunfire did little to send them fleeing.

Spence ran around a long bend in the road and to his right he could hear the rumble of the Salmon River. "I'm getting close," he thought with a tinge of hope. He and Chuck went fishing every summer in the Salmon River, which flowed next to town. He dared to glance back and gasped to find the giant Bigfoot gaining, only thirty feet away. With the last of his energy, he burst into the fastest sprint he could muster. "I'm not going to make it," he thought in horror.

Spence tried running faster, but could not, his body quickly losing what little energy he had left as he gasped for air, his lungs burning, and his legs sluggish. The heavy footsteps of the Bigfoot grew louder and closer behind him, never wavering. The Bigfoot closed the distance to 15 feet. Up ahead, houses appeared along the sides of the road meaning he had reached the outskirts of the north end of town. Lights were on in the houses, but no one was outside to help him. Spence ran, his body weak, his lungs wheezing for air. He slipped on a slick section of the road and would have fallen but he managed to right himself and keep running.

"Help me," he screamed in a horse voice between gasps. "Help." The Bigfoot growled behind him sounding even closer. "Help," Spence yelled in panic expecting to feel the monster's hands grab him at any second.

The Scout ran after the manthing, enjoying the chase. It could have caught up to its prey much earlier, but it was amused by the chase. The manthing had tried all evening to escape, but there was no escape. The tide had finally been turned, as the hunter now became the hunted. Its hiding and starvation was over and its fury would be unleashed upon its enemies.

With a burst of speed, the Scout surged forward grabbing the manthing by the shoulder and knocking him to the ground. The manthing yelled and struggled as the Scout attacked, pounding with its giant fists. The manthings blows barely even registered in the Scout's mind as it growled and smashed its prey's head into the ground. It broke the manthing's neck and stood up roaring victoriously. The Scout's brothers approached from behind as it gazed down the road at the manthings' dwellings. It raised its head and gave the signal, a loud, high-pitched, apish shriek. It had already sent a group of its brothers to the south end of town. There would be no escape as a chorus of shrills, shrieks and roars filled the surrounding woods. Dozens of Sasquatch advanced on Hyder.

CHAPTER 6

Stephen Denmin drove a Ford Explorer out of the south end of Hyder towards Stewart, Canada, which was two miles away. In the passenger seat, Victor Morey sat with an agitated scowl on his face as he crossed his arms. In the back seat sat three of his employees, Henry, Joe and Greg, part of his Sasquatch Team, trained in all types of weaponry and armed with guns, explosives, cameras and every high tech device he could afford.

A sullen expression framed Stephen's face. His demeanor showed impatience with frustration brimming to the surface. He was eager to eat his steak and plan the next few days. They had been staking out the entrances to a few old abandoned mines today, setting up cameras and motion-detecting devices. They were also doing research through a satellite link trying to map every mine, which was a daunting task. This had been mining country eighty years ago, but by the early 1950s nearly all the mines had closed. The boom had been in the 1920s, the crash in the 1930s with the onset of the great depression. After that, many of the companies that had mined the area no longer existed and their records lost. No one knew how many forgotten mines were in this isolated area, but he had to find out.

His Sasquatch, the group that had killed his wife, were most likely hiding in one of the mines in the area. Where else could they be? He had flown planes and helicopters over hundreds of square miles with infrared, heat sensing equipment. These bastards had killed his wife at their cabin four years ago and then disappeared, slipping away from one of the biggest searches ever mounted. This frustrated Stephen more than anything. He did not like to lose and when it came to the Sasquatch he swore he would stop them, get revenge and experiment on them with the help of Victor. He thought of his cabin that had burned down when the Sasquatch had attacked. The place had always been his refuge, isolated from everything on a mountain lake surrounded by miles upon miles of forest. It had been his secret locale where he escaped the fast paced life of running a business, getting away from all the day-to-day struggles and just relaxing far from civilization with his wife. The cabin was where he could always catch his breath and reflect on life without having to answer faxes, phone calls, text messages and emails. He had bought the cabin as a present to Claire and they had gone up there for years spending quality time together, but now he would never return to that place. The Sasquatch had desecrated his refuge by murdering his wife and burning down his cabin. He gritted his teeth at the thought and squeezed the steering wheel forcing out the pent up tension. He was ready to strike out and make those monsters pay with blood. For the last four years Stephen's whole life had been dedicated to the sole purpose of finding those bastards. He had sold most of his mining company and funneled millions into accomplishing this goal.

Stephen suddenly slammed on the brakes, the Explorer skidding to a stop. "What the hell?"

In front of them a barricade of trees blocked the road. It looked like the trees had been cracked at the base and knocked down. The branches concealed the road ahead and he could not tell how many trees had fallen.

"What happened here?" Victor asked in an annoyed voice. "Can you drive around it?"

Stephen parked the car, got out and shined a flashlight. To the right, a gully lined one side of the road and to the left all the trees were knocked over and beyond that was the forest. A cold wind gusted through the branches of the surrounding trees. "We're stuck. Hey Greg, can you walk up to the Canadian Customs and let them know about this. It's about a five-minute walk from here. Hopefully they have some equipment that can move this crap."

"Okay," Greg said and got out of the car with his backpack full of weapons and explosives. "What the hell happened here? Looks like a tornado touched down."

Stephen shook his head. "I have no idea… some practical joke? Some freak weather?"

"What are we going to do?" Victor asked with a scowl on his face.

"We sit here and wait to hear back from Greg." Stephen got back into the vehicle, turned up the heat and put on his favorite country CD. "We may have to walk back to our hotel."

"Almost two miles away," Victor snapped with a perturbed look in his eyes.

"And damn cold," Stephen said laughing. "Why does crap like this have to happen?"

Greg, a 35-year-old Canadian, who had worked for Stephen for three years, clicked on his flashlight and shined it on the pile of fallen trees. There was no way in hell he was going to climb over that mess, with all the branches sticking straight up. Many trees were on top of each other making a near impossible barrier to climb. He moved the beam of light to his left alongside the road where a dark wall of towering trees stood. Some of the trees close to the road had been knocked down, the trunks splintered.

Greg turned to the right where the drainage ditch dropped down alongside the road. It was rocky with patches of ice, and many of the tops of the tree and branches hung over the ditch, creating a makeshift tunnel. He decided to go this way since it looked the easiest. Greg climbed down into the ditch, shined his light ahead, branches blocking much of the view and started walking. The branches swayed in the wind making creaking noises and creating shadows that danced back and forth in the beam of his flashlight. He ducked under a thick branch and moved quickly. Tired and cold from a long day out in the woods, Greg wanted to get this over with as quickly as possible, so he could eat, drink beer and crash in his warm bed.

"I can't complain," he whispered as he brushed through more branches and slipped on a slick rock. Stephen paid well and the job allowed him to travel and hike through a lot of beautiful remote places. Not many people could claim to be a Sasquatch hunter full time for a living. He wasn't chained to a desk eight hours a day staring at a computer like a zombie. He had tried that once and nearly went insane with boredom, restlessness and headaches. He liked to be outdoors, free, moving around doing different tasks each day.

Greg pushed through the swaying, creaking branches at a quick pace. About halfway down the ditch, a branch snapped to his left, making a loud cracking sound, almost as if something had stepped on it. Greg stopped and shined his light into the overhead branches, unable to see much within the mass of fallen trees. He shined the light back and forth and continued down the ditch. "The trees must still be settling," he thought unperturbed. He reached the end of the barricade and climbed back out onto the road.

Greg flashed his light on the barricade behind him shaking his head with disbelief. "What happened here?" He whispered finding it unbelievable. "A freak wind storm? Construction? Loggers?" He suddenly remembered a report about the "Ape Cave Horror" how the Sasquatch had knocked down several trees and stuffed them into the entrance of the Ape Cave to trap the people within.

"But it was nothing on this scale of destruction," he thought. "They can't be that strong. Some of the trees are massive and so many. I'm just spooking myself."

Troubled, Greg walked briskly down the road, anxious to get back to the car. The wind blew in heavy gusts and the trees all around swayed and creaked in the night. Clouds covered most of the dark sky and only a few stars were visible. He walked around a bend in the road and up ahead was the brightly lit Canadian Customs, which was nothing more than a white rectangular, one-story mobile house with a separate wooden roof built over it so when cars stopped, the people would have some protection from the rain. A Canadian flag flapped loudly on a pole near the building.

As Greg approached, he slowed down, as a worried looked descended upon his face. Someone was lying motionless on the ground near the side of the building. The worry turned to fear as he noticed a window was shattered, bits of glass dotted the pavement. Greg walked over to the body glancing back and forth with trepidation as the wind gusted and the trees swayed making him feel even more isolated. He kneeled down and looked at the body as recognition filled his eyes. It was the customs border lady who had checked them through earlier today as she did almost everyday when they left the hotel in Stewart to go the Hyder. She always had a jolly expression on her face, laughing and talking loudly, asking how their hunt for Bigfoot was going. But now the jolliness was gone, replaced with a cold, terror frozen in her wide, dead eyes. Her neck was broken and her shirt was wet with blood around her stomach as if something had slashed her.

Greg stood up and pulled out his 9 mm handgun. About 40 feet down the road towards Stewart, an overturned truck lay on its side. He walked to the front of the Customs building and winced. The whole front wall had been smashed inwards. Greg clicked the safety off of his gun and stepped through the gaping hole. Inside, the office looked like a war zone with furniture smashed and strewn papers everywhere. In the back room was the body of the other customs official, a man in his mid fifties he had talked to many times.

Greg phoned Stephen as he glanced back and forth in a panic. "Something big is going on here. The customs' building was attacked. There's a huge hole in the wall and the two custom agents are dead."

"Get your ass back here," Stephen said. "I'll call the authorities."

Greg hung up and stepped through the hole in the wall to the outside where a cold wind greeted him, brushing past his pale face. All around, in every direction was a dark wall of trees leading to miles and miles of wilderness. This time the forest looked different, ominous, foreboding, threatening, hiding its secrets. Was something watching him this very minute? Greg shined his flashlight around, but the beam seemed too weak as the darkness swallowed it. The branches swung, creaking in the wind as if they had life of their own trying to reach out and pull him into the black of the woods. Some of the bushes moved on the fringes of the tree line looking like monstrous humanoid shapes. Greg ran up the road leaving the bright lights of the Customs Building behind, back into the dark of night.

"Was it Bigfoot?" he thought in distress as terror began to build. What else could it have been? He reached the barricade, a massive shadowy clump of intertwined branches. "Almost there," he thought as he jumped down into the drainage ditch. Greg moved as quickly as he could with his gun in one hand and the flashlight in the other, ducking under the thicker branches and pushing through the smaller ones. "If this barricade was caused by Bigfoot, we're screwed," Greg thought finding this almost unreal.

In a sudden blur of motion, branches burst apart as something huge and dark surged forward from within the fallen trees, knocking Greg to the ground. He managed one shot from his handgun that struck the ground before the Sasquatch smashed him with a deadly blow to the face. The beast began to bite into him. Blood splattered on the ground as the Bigfoot began to feast.

"Did you hear that?" Victor asked, looking out the passenger door window.

"Gunfire," Stephen said from the driver's seat and flipped off the music. He called Greg's cell phone but there was no answer.

"Go back to Hyder," Victor said, his voice cracking with anxiety.

Henry and Joe, who sat in the back seat, pulled out their guns.

Deep growling caused Stephen to look out the driver's window, his eyes growing wide as a giant shadowy, figure charged across the road and slammed into the side of the Explorer. The whole vehicle flipped over, rolling into the drainage ditch. All around the overturned vehicle, the shrieking cries of the Sasquatch broke the quiet of the forest. Dark shapes emerged from the undergrowth and began to advance upon the vehicle.

CHAPTER 7

"Do you know where I can get the location of some of the old mines from the 20s and 30s?" Andrew asked the bartender as he sipped his martini. He liked the bar and had decided to order another drink after Chad left. He felt at home here and did not like being alone in his room at the inn. Too many dark thoughts of regret and sadness plagued him when he was alone.

The bartender shrugged his shoulders. "There are mines all over up in the mountains and down in the valleys. I would check the Stewart Public Library. I'm sure they'll have some information. They have stacks of old papers and records. You think the Bigfoots are hiding in a mine?"

"Sasquatch," Andrew corrected with an annoyed tone. "Possibly a mine or some cave." He popped another olive in his mouth, missing his old team. He still found it hard to believe that they were all dead: his daughter Sherrie; Javier, who worked for him for 17 years; Enrique, just a boy; and Donald, his tech guy. His thoughts were always drawn towards them and soon after, feelings of guilt would surface. He had prohibited his team from carrying weapons absolutely convinced that the Sasquatch were peaceful creatures. Chad had even warned him of their true nature, but his bull-headed stubbornness prevented him from listening. He remembered his arrogance, thinking that he was the expert, not Chad, feeling some sort of resentment and jealously for the young man who had actually seen the animal. Andrew had spent 40 years looking for this legendary creature and then Chad found them on some random trip to Canada. That had infuriated him for a long time. He should have been the first to discover this new species, but that was a long time ago and now he knew better. Chad was now one of his only friends.

"I'm an old fool," Andrew thought. "An old, lonely fool." His face creased with anger as he forced back those unwanted feelings and much too painful memories. He could not dwell in the past or he would go crazy. He had a job to do and so much to accomplish and learn about these secretive animals. He was at the forefront of Sasquatch research and intended to stay that way. If he could capture one he would be able to trump all the other so-called experts.

Andrew stood up with a groan, his right knee aching. "Watch my drink will you," he said to the bartender. He grabbed his cane and walked to the restroom in the back of the bar. His cane was fairly new, made by the same man in Tacoma who had made the first one. His original cane had been broken deep in the hidden caves by Mount Saint Helens. This cane was carved out of Mahogany with a silver, metal hand, the head shaped like a Sasquatch with its hands clutched together as if it was reaching out straight ahead. It was much more expensive than his original cane which he thought he deserved after all the bullcrap he had gone through over the last couple years.

Andrew used the restroom, washed his hands and looked in the mirror. His eyes were bloodshot with tired, heavy bags under them. The lines on his face seemed deeper and the skin sagged more than ever, pale and dry with age spots from spending most of his life outdoors. "It's a bitch getting old," he whispered as he felt time slipping through his fingers. He still had a lifetime of research to finish and he had just started with the recovery of the Sasquatch corpses at Mount Saint Helens. They still knew so little about these animals. How intelligent were they? He had witnessed the communication directly when the Grandfather, the old, white haired Sasquatch, had made hand gestures and grunting noises. The Grandfather had displayed fear, curiosity and anger. "Whatever happened to that old bugger?" He had stabbed it in the stomach and left it in the cave. Afterwards, those caves were thoroughly searched by the police but the Grandfather was never found. "I hope you made it my dear friend," he thought. The Grandfather had seemed the most harmless of all of them.

The bodies of the Grandfather, the Father, the Mother as well as at least three or four live Sasquatch had vanished. Where did they go? Andrew surmised that they were still near Mount Saint Helens hidden away in some deep cave that they had not discovered yet.

A loud ruckus of yells, cries of fear, crashing sounds as if tables were being overturned and glass breaking in the bar pulled Andrew from his thoughts. Andrew walked towards the door to leave the restroom to investigate what was going on in the other room, but he suddenly stopped turning rigid, his mouth gaping open and his eyes growing wide with recognition. A loud ferocious roar bellowed from the bar, so loud that the yells of the men seemed like quiet whispers.

"A Sasquatch," Andrew rasped in utter shock and took a step back away from the restroom door. An uncontrollable trembling moved through his body as he took steps back further into the restroom, his knuckles white as he clutched the handle of his cane. Men were yelling and screaming as the roars and growling continued loudly. "At least two of them are here," he whispered. He shuddered as conflicting emotions stormed through his mind. He had spent his entire adult life searching for the Sasquatch hoping to capture one even after the events of the "Ape Cave Horror." His goal had never been to kill these rare beasts, but to study them. This species was few in numbers and each time one died it brought them closer to extinction. The tranquilizer guns were back at the hotel, but did he even want to use them? His back pressed against the far wall of the restroom next to the stall as he stared at the door as the clamor continued. His breathing grew heavy and his heart raced as the sounds of battle intensified. A loud thump shook the wall as if somebody had been thrown against it.

The cries of the men were swiftly silenced and the bathroom door flew open with a loud bang. A Sasquatch, tall, hairy, mouth opened revealing jagged teeth, stepped in the doorway, hunched over to fit through. Its dark eyes zoomed in on Andrew who winced back against the wall.

With no hesitation, Andrew drew his handgun and fired, hot anger creasing his face. He struck the beast in the arm and stomach and kept firing. Andrew yelled in an uncontrollable rage, his eye turning to madness as he kept pulling the trigger. The Sasquatch stumbled back into the bar, the restroom door swinging shut. He fired three more times before he managed to quell the madness smoldering inside his mind.

"You killed my daughter," Andrew rasped in a burst of hot anger and leaned back against the wall, exhausted and breathing hard as he continued to point the gun at the door. His ears rang from the deafening gunfire; the bar had gone eerily quiet. All the talk of capturing one of these monsters left him the moment he saw the

Sasquatch enter the bathroom. It was the first one he had seen since the "Ape Cave Horror." The last time, the Sasquatch had killed his daughter. He had never felt so angry as he stood against the restroom wall, his chin tight, and his eyes livid with hatred.

Even though rage surged through his mind like crashing waves, questions began to seep in, begging for answers. Why did the Sasquatch attack? Where did they come from? How did it manage to reach town and attack the very bar he was in? What were the odds? A Sasquatch had never entered a town before, let alone attack a bar full of people. Were there more than just one? He was sure he had heard at least two. Had his bullets manage to kill it? All was uncomfortably silent in the bar. Despite his fear, he had to go investigate.

He took a step and stopped abruptly. He heard heavy footsteps and grunting sounds. More glass broke and a chair was knocked over. Andrew went rigid and held his breath, his eyes wide as he listened. The footsteps thumped on the floor, creaking underneath its weight. Andrew held the gun aimed at the door squeezing it tightly. All went silent moments later. Andrew waited at the back of the restroom for several minutes.

Gathering enough fortitude and what little valor he had, Andrew took a step towards the door. A stern, determined expression settled on his face, while his beaded eyes looked ahead for danger as he took another step. His cane clicked on the floor as he kept his gun aimed in front of him. The silence was deafening. What had happened to everyone? Where were the Sasquatch? What the hell was going on? Why was it so quiet? He wanted to yell at the top of his lungs, but he kept his teeth clenched. He reached the door and opened it slowly to find the entire bar empty. All the tables and chairs were knocked over and broken glasses and bottles were everywhere. Jackets and hats were strewn on the floor. The Sasquatch as well as everyone that had been in the bar were nowhere to be seen.

Andrew kneeled down and examined a blood streak that made a straight line towards the front door. He noticed other blood streaks, all of them pointing towards the front door, which had been knocked off its hinges. "Looks like they dragged the bodies outside. Where the hell did the beast go? I shot it several times." A cold wind blew into the bar dispelling the warm, cozy feel in the room. He put on his coat, which was crumpled on the floor and noticed his martini shattered by the foot of the chair he had been sitting on. Andrew walked slowly to the front door and aimed his gun. He stepped out onto the porch and froze. A giant, shadowy figure raced across the street disappearing in between two houses. A high-pitched apish wail blared through the night sky, followed by other monstrous roars. Gunfire went off and screams and yells of men and women could be heard in the distance.

"They're everywhere," Andrew rasped in shock stepping back into the bar. "The Sasquatch are attacking the entire town." He reached into his coat and pulled out his cell phone and tried calling Chad but it went to voicemail. He rang Stephen and Alberto, but no one answered.

"Not again," Andrew whispered.

Outside he heard, heavy footsteps on the gravel road approaching the front door of the bar followed by deep growling. Andrew shuffled to the back of the bar. Apish clicking noises snorted loudly as the footsteps thumped upon the porch. "They're coming back," he thought in panic.

Andrews's eyes were drawn to the back door near the restroom. He hurried across the room as quietly as he could and opened the door, stepping outside into darkness. There was a shed in the back yard. Just then, a loud roar erupted as crashing sounds came from within the bar.

Andrew scrambled around to the side of the bar where another building stood creating a narrow walkway. There was a loud clamor in the store next to him as furniture was toppled and thrashed around. He could hear growling in both buildings.

"There's no escape," Andrew uttered in desperation, trying to quell the panic he felt growing inside. He kneeled down in the blackness of the night in the narrow walkway between the two buildings uncertain of what to do, but hide. He looked towards the street where a dim streetlight gave off a pale, yellowish light. Dark, beastly shapes bounded back and forth across the road. Andrew sat huddled in the shadows with a grim look on his face and waited as he listened to the ungodly roars of the Sasquatch and the screams of their victims.

CHAPTER 8

Chad stood on the porch of the general store, a cold wind brushing across his tense face, as he stared down the empty street listening for what he prayed he would never hear again. He was visibly shaken and was gripping the railing, his knuckles white. His chest was tight and his stomach felt upset. He could have sworn he had heard the scream of a Sasquatch, but how could that be possible? They would never venture into town. They avoided man. Chad shook his head trying to get a grip on his fear and took a deep breath. Except for the wind rustling through the branches, all was quiet. "It must have been something else," he thought. "They would never come to town."

A shrieking, monstrous cry broke the still, somewhere down the road on the northside of town. Chad winced, clenched his teeth and visibly shook with terror. He looked in the direction of the horrifying sound and saw dark shadowy, man-like shapes, lumbering up the street towards his position. Chad hurried back into the building, locking the door behind him, his hands trembling, his stomach tightening into a knot. All color had drained from his face. He held the door handle for several moments, making sure it was locked as he listened to the nightmarish sounds that were quickly getting closer.

"What are you doing?" Mrs. Measly asked from behind the cash register.

Chad turned around and faced her with fearful eyes. "They're here… the Sasquatch." He pulled out his glock. "They're in town."

"What?" Mrs. Measly asked in a troubled, unsure voice, her eyes growing wide, warily looking at the gun. A loud roar bellowed from somewhere nearby close to the building, rising with a deep, ferocious tone, so loud that Chad went rigid and gasped. Even Mrs. Measly, with her bad hearing, heard the sound causing her to drop a notebook she had been holding. The Sasquatch's roar continued to rise turning into a high-pitched, shrieking wail.

Both Chad and Mrs. Measly froze as the roar crested and began to fade. They looked fearfully at the door. Whatever monstrous creature had made that noise was outside the front of the store, possibly only a few feet away. Panic gripped Chad making his stomach feel increasingly queasy. Stepping away from the door with images of beastly hands breaking through to grab him, Chad winced when he heard apish grunts along the side of the building. He had not heard that hellish sound for over a year. His breathing quickened and grew shallow as his mouth gaped open. The last time was at Mount Saint Helens, when the Father, the biggest Sasquatch he had ever seen, killed Sherrie and would have gotten him too if Andrew had not arrived on the scene. Whenever he had heard that nightmarish scream, it had meant death for many people.

"Crimmeny," Mrs. Measly gasped. "Is it really a Bigfoot? Is it a joke?" As if in answer, a Sasquatch shrieked loud and harsh. "How many are there?" Mrs. Measly cried with sudden urgency.

Loud pounding and banging began against the back of the store, the powerful blows sounding like a battering ram was smashing the wall. It grew louder as wood cracked followed by a thundering boom as an entire section of the wall collapsed and burst inwards. The whole building shook and merchandise crashed onto the floor down the aisle, glass shattering in the windows.

Chad dashed to the cash register, grabbed Mrs. Measly's hand and headed for the stairs that led to the second level. "They're inside," Chad rasped. Growling could be heard in the back of the store as several Bigfoot climbed through the hole. Chad helped Mrs. Measly up the stairs. "Is this the only way up here?"

Mrs. Measly nodded, her eyes wide with fear behind her glasses.

"Good, we should be safe up here. If they try for the stairs, I'll shoot them. Go get your grandson. Bring guns if you have them." Chad stopped at the top of the stairs and crouched down as Mrs. Measly scampered off. He took a deep breath and aimed his gun towards the steps below. "I don't want to see them again," he whispered, while the growls and crashing sounds grew nearer as the Bigfoot demolished the entire first level. The front door smashed open as a Bigfoot entered, its steps making loud thumps against the floor. "I can't panic," he said between clenched teeth. "Keep a clear mind and a steady hand." He knew the Sasquatch were quick and crafty and he could not make any mistakes.

Mrs. Measly and her grandson rushed up to Chad carrying rifles; both of them had spooked looks stretched across their faces. Chad glanced briefly in their direction and then turned back around and gasped in fright. At the base of the stairs stood a Sasquatch glaring up at Chad with black rage-filled eyes. It was massive, with a thick, muscular frame covered in shaggy brown hair, over seven feet in height. Chad had forgotten how frightening these monsters appeared up close. The Bigfoot launched forward with surprising speed, lurching up the stairs, its clawed hands out-stretched to strike. Chad yelled and unloaded the entire clip into the Bigfoot as it reached within a foot of him before falling back down the stairs.

"Shoot, shoot, shoot, shoot, shoot," Chad cursed, reaching into his coat pocket for a new clip with his sweaty hands.

Mrs. Measly had dropped her rifle, utterly shocked by the frightening appearance of a Bigfoot close up. "We have to get out of here," she cried, her voice drowned by the wails of the Sasquatch and the destruction of her store.

"Don't worry Grandma," Eric said.

Chad loaded the new clip and stared down at the Sasquatch lying at the bottom of the stairs, blood oozing from various wounds. "Its still breathing," he rasped, fear lining his voice. "How could it still be alive after so many gunshots," he thought and aimed for the head, putting the beast out of its misery.

Another Bigfoot appeared near the corpse, but jumped back out of sight as Chad blasted away. "They learn fast," he muttered as a terrifying thought grabbed him, bringing the panic bubbling back up into his mind. What if the Bigfoot had come here for him? What if they were attacking the town to specifically kill him? He was the only one to escape the massacre at Camp Elizabeth. Were these the same Sasquatch? Had they seen him hiking in the woods during the last three weeks? Was it possible that these creatures were capable of revenge? Could they actually remember him from four years ago? Was that even a realistic thought? He had also escaped the Ape Caves, where a few of the Bigfoot had vanished afterwards. Did those Bigfoot journey up to Canada? Were they now part of this larger group?

"No," he thought and shook his head trying to reassure himself. "They're animals, dumb brutes that kill. The concept of revenge was impossible." He looked down at the dead Sasquatch as the memories of the last four years flooded back into his mind as pure fear. He took several deep breaths. "Be strong."

Growling and heavy footsteps drew nearer somewhere on the first level. Outside he could hear gunshots and the occasional yells and screams of men and woman, which were overpowered by the deafening roars of the Sasquatch. "They must be everywhere," Chad thought.

With no warning, the cash register hurled through the air crashing halfway up the stairs. Startled, Chad cried out and fell back and fired. He quickly righted himself as the cash register clanged down the steps.

"My store," Mr. Measly gasped. "This is all I have and those things are destroying it."

"Don't worry Grandma," Eric said.

"Call for help, call the police," Chad yelled as he stayed perched at the top of the stairs.

"There's no police in Hyder. If we need a law officer, it takes them a 45 minute flight from another city."

"Call them anyways," Chad snapped. "What about Stewart? The Canadians?

"They have a couple officers."

"Call them too… we need as much help as possible." Chad kept his eyes focused down the stairs the entire time he spoke.

"Ok, ok," Mrs. Measly said, getting some restraint on the terror she felt. A window shattered on the second level near the back by the sub shop.

"They're climbing through the window," Eric yelled. "Stay with Chad, Grandma. I love you."

"Don't go," Mrs. Measly cried as her grandson dashed off down an aisle. Gunfire boomed as Eric fired his rifle.

The entire stairwell began to shake and crack. The walls started to burst inwards as the Sasquatch pounded into the structure from below. Chad leaned against one of the walls trying to steady himself as the floor shook. Mrs. Measly fell down, dropping her rifle a second time.

"My store," Mrs. Measly cried out. "My husband spent 35 years running it before he died."

"Keep quiet," Chad yelled as one side of the stairwell, cracked, wood splintering everywhere. A thick, hairy fist broke through and withdrew. Gunfire continued to thunder near the sub shop as Eric fired at the Bigfoot trying to climb in through the windows. The stairwell cracked again and a monstrous fist broke through creating another gaping hole. Chad fired, off balance, and missed as the hand withdrew. "Call for help," Chad commanded as their situation quickly deteriorated. Mrs. Measly, who still lay on the floor, fished out a cell phone and tried dialing a number as the building rattled like an earthquake had struck.

Suddenly, the stairwell shook with the most violent impact so far; the entire bottom half of the stairs cracked in two and collapsed. Chad fell back and lost the grip of his glock, which clanked across the floor. Chad lunged for the gun as Mrs. Measly yelled in terror, falling on her back when the building swayed.

Eric screamed and went silent. Seconds later, three Bigfoot emerged from the aisles behind them on the top level. With no hesitation, Chad yelled and fired the glock, lying on his stomach, sending a barrage of bullets at the advance. The beasts retreated back into the aisles for cover.

"We have to get out here," Chad yelled as the entire floor buckled. He stood up and moved over to Mrs. Measly who was unable to get her balance and was now lying on her stomach.

"My grandson," Mrs. Measly cried. "Where is he? Eric, come back here... Eric."

A Bigfoot stepped from behind the far aisle to the left and flung a microwave directly at Chad, who ducked, dropping to the floor. The microwave missed his head by inches and crashed against the wall behind him. Chad raised the glock, gunfire thundered, striking the beast in the shoulder and arm before it leaped back for cover.

Behind Chad, a Bigfoot climbed up the ruined remains of the stairwell, its claws stabbing deep into the wood near the top. Chad grabbed Mrs. Measly's hand and pulled her to her feet. They moved away from the stairwell to a corner where at least they would not be surrounded.

"Call for help," Chad yelled.

"But my grandson," Mrs. Measly sobbed.

"Call for help or we'll all be dead." Chad turned to see two of the Sasquatch peering from the aisles. He fired at them forcing them to back off.

A hairy, clawed hand struck the floor at the top of the stairwell as a Sasquatch pulled itself up. Chad fired, striking its arm. The beast fell back tumbling down the ruined remains of the stairs. The other three Bigfoot, hidden in the aisles, charged in a blur of motion, letting loose shrieking war cries. Chad managed to shoot one down before the other two reached his position. Their heavy blows fell like cement bricks as they pummeled him.

As darkness overtook Chad, he heard Mrs. Measly scream.

CHAPTER 9

Stephen Denmin bumped his head knocking himself out as the Explorer rolled into the drainage ditch. The others were battered and thrashed around from the crash. The vehicle came to a stop upside down. Victor, who sat in the passenger seat, found himself on his side in a ball. He sat up and tried to push open the door, but it was jammed against a rock. The entire forest seemed to come alive as the Sasquatch advanced on them. Heavy footsteps thumped in the night through the undergrowth near the road as vegetation was trampled, branches creaked and foliage crunched.

Henry and Tim, who were upside down in the back seat, clicked off their seatbelts and twisted around to sit up. They pulled out their glocks, both of them with spooked looks on their faces. A Sasquatch charged across the road and leaped up into the air over the drainage ditch, smashing down on top of the vehicle. The entire Explorer shook violently upon impact, glass cracking and windows shattering. The Bigfoot jumped up and down as if it were trying to crush them into the ground. Metal creaked as the box of the Explorer squished down several inches unable to withstand the onslaught.

Henry yelled defiantly, scooted over to the window, and stuck his hand out pointed up and blindly blasted with his glock. Tim kicked out his window and shot from the other side. A beastly, hairy hand reached down grabbing at Tim, but he pulled his arm back into the safety of the vehicle.

"There's one on top," Victor cried, his mouth gaped opened as he frantically glanced back and forth in a panic.

"Really?" Henry snapped and stuck the glock back out the window aiming up, hoping to clip the beast. The Bigfoot jumped off the Explorer back onto the road, causing the carriage to drop a couple more inches, like stepping on a soda can. "Victor, help Stephen."

Victor moved over and unhooked Stephen's seatbelt. After much struggling, he managed to turn Stephen upright. Their boss started groaning. Meanwhile, Tim crawled out of his window and stood up, peppering the road with bullets. A Bigfoot leaped for cover behind some of the fallen trees that had formed the blockade. Another Bigfoot backed up to the far side of the road, disappearing into the foliage.

"Hurry," Tim yelled. "It's clear. We can't get trapped in here."

Henry climbed across the seat and out of Tim's window so both of them were on the same side of the vehicle. "Watch out," Henry cried as the trunk of a tree, like some black shadow, hurdled through the air and smashed on top of the truck. Both of them dropped down, ducking. The trunk bounced off and landed in the ditch.

"What's going on?" Stephen mumbled, opening his eyes and squinting in a daze.

"We've got to get out of here," Victor yelled as he climbed into the back seat gripping a handgun and a flashlight. Groggily, Stephen followed.

Henry and Tim stood up, both blasting away towards the road. The apish grunts and shrill cries of the Sasquatch filled the woods all around them. "Victor, help Stephen out of the car," Henry yelled between bursts of gunfire.

"What do you think I'm doing?" Victor shot back. Branches snapped right behind them. Henry reacted immediately; twirling around to see a Sasquatch emerge from the bushes, arms raised with claws ready to strike. Henry unloaded an entire clip into the monster before the beast stumbled back collapsing on the ground. Tim kept shooting towards the road. Henry changed clips in seconds and then sprayed a whole clip of bullets into the tree line behind them making sure no others were stalking them in that direction.

"I'm coming out," Victor yelled from inside the Explorer. Henry sidestepped out of the way so Victor could climb out the window followed by Stephen who had blood dripping from a gash on his forehead. Both Victor and Stephen stood up with flashlights and glocks.

"You okay?" Henry asked.

Stephen nodded and wiped his forehead. "Looks like we hit the jackpot. Victor call Greg; he's out there alone."

"No answer," Victor said tersely a few seconds later.

"Shoot, we'll have to look for him after we get this situation under control." Stephen began firing his glock toward the road where the shrill apish screams were concentrated. Henry rushed around the truck and climbed up the side of the ditch and peeked over. The road was pitch black, so he shined a flashlight and found a

Bigfoot running across the road towards him holding a rock over its head. Henry dropped down yelling, "Incoming."

The rock whizzed by within inches of his head crashing against the top of the Explorer and nearly striking Victor who fell to the ground in fright. Stephen sent a barrage of gunfire at the beast, but it had already rushed back into the darkness. Henry crawled up the ditch again and fired from the left to the right, hoping to hit any that dared cross the road. A Sasquatch squealed in pain somewhere in the black.

Wood cracked, thundering loudly, behind them before an entire tree fell on top of the Explorer. Everyone dropped down and luckily the trunk missed them, but still the branches scratched and scraped them. Victor cried out. Henry pushed his way through the tangle of branches and moved around to the back end of the Explorer where Tim joined him. They both fired into the trees and then turned and shot across the road. Stephen and Victor crawled out from under the branches cursing.

"We need to get to higher ground," Henry gasped. "Up on the road. At least it's open up there and they won't be able to sneak up on us."

"Let's do it," Stephen yelled, and while the others climbed up out of the ditch, he opened the back window of the Explorer pulling out a container of gasoline. There were few gas stations in the area so they always brought along some of their own when driving on the old roads that weaved through the hills and forests. Stephen opened the lid and quickly poured the gasoline around the back of the Explorer. He dropped the container and clicked on his lighter and flung it to the ground. A line of fire flared up several feet into the air illuminating the perimeter around them.

Stephen climbed out of the ditch and rushed to the center of the road joining the others, all of them flashing their lights back and forth along the tree line.

"Good idea," Henry said.

The light from the fire revealed a Sasquatch crawling towards them only a few feet away from the ditch. The beast seemed surprised by the sudden fire, jumped up and retreated back into the tree line.

"Damn... we're surrounded." Stephen cursed. "Form a circle." Back to back, they stood, facing all directions as the fire flicked shadows across the road. Lights shined and bullets blasted, all of them tense and nervous. Stephen wiped the blood out of his eyes dripping from the gash on his forehead. Branches cracking and the rustle of bushes could be heard as the Sasquatch circled them in the undergrowth.

"Stay cool everyone," Stephen yelled. "If they come out in the open, blast hell out of them."

The roars continued for several minutes and then stopped all at once, followed by an unnerving silence. Stephen signaled them to end the shooting to conserve ammo. Their ears were ringing from the gunfire as they stood, breathing heavily, shining their flashlights around the eerily quiet forest.

Minutes went by and then Stephen huffed, "I think its clear."

"It could be a trap," Henry warned.

"Maybe, but we have to work fast. Let's find Greg." Stephen led them towards the barricade of trees that lined the road. He called Greg's cell phone and in the distance a ringing could be heard. "His cell is close by. Follow me." Stephen climbed down into the drainage ditch and pushed through the branches shining his flashlight ahead. Victor followed close behind with fear and trepidation striking his tense face. Henry walked along the top of the ditch near the tree line. Tim took the endpoint, staying in the ditch and glancing back periodically.

In front of them, a flashlight, like a beacon, shined on the ground. Stephen rushed over and found Greg's cell phone and rifle. There were spots of wet blood on some of the rocks. "Shoot. Looks like those bastards got him."

Dismayed, everyone looked around with distraught faces. Greg had worked with them for two years and had been a great friend. Stephen and Greg had gone drinking many times telling crazy stories.

"We have to find him," Henry demanded. "He might still be alive."

Stephen nodded. "We will." They moved back out of the ditch and onto the road. Stephen called Chad, Andrew, and Alberto, but no one answered. "What the hell is happening? We need to find out the extent of this invasion. Also, time is of the essence. It will be at least an hour before the authorities can fly here and tomorrow before they will be able to be here in force. Call the chopper. We're going Bigfoot hunting."

CHAPTER 10

Andrew crouched down in the safety of the darkness between the bar and another building as he listened to the devastation all around and watched fearfully as several hulking dark shapes rushed along the main road. His mind reeled from this sudden attack trying to come up with some conclusion, answers to the nightmare that had beset Hyder. He gripped his handgun in one hand and his cane in the other. The terror he felt paralyzed him as he hid away, while curiosity crawled through his mind. Only once before, at Camp Elizabeth, had such a large number of Sasquatch attacked a human settlement. Bewilderment fluttered through his head as he tried to comprehend why these creatures had invaded this town. For all of recorded history the Sasquatch had remained hidden, mysterious animals, keeping to themselves, but something had changed. Was it just this group of Sasquatch, most likely the same ones that had attacked Camp Elizabeth, which had become so violent and aggressive? The few Sasquatch near Mount Saint Helens had been starving; one factor in their violent behavior, not to mention that he had intruded into their lair. But these Sasquatch in Alaska were different. They were becoming bolder. What had caused this change of behavior? What was their purpose? It could not just be blatant rampage and destruction.

Andrew's cell phone rang, startling him, sounding so loud and harsh in the quiet of his hideaway. The phone rang a second time as he fumbled in his jacket in desperate panic. He pulled it out and saw Stephen's name flashing on it. Clicking it off immediately, he stuffed the phone in his pocket. "At least they're okay," he thought, looking apprehensively at the road hoping the phone had not betrayed his position. "I hope Chad and Alberto are safe. The entire town must be under attack. How many Sasquatch were out there?"

From inside the building he was huddling next to, a loud apish grunting could be heard. It stopped suddenly after Andrew's phone rang. The beast breathed slowly and began sniffing. Andrew went rigid. Heavy footsteps beat against the floor growing nearer. The wood creaked underneath the monster's massive weight.

Andrew squeezed the handle of his gun, not daring to stand up and run. Where would he go? The beasts were everywhere and he had no chance of outrunning them. The footsteps drew nearer to the wall where he was kneeled down next to and then they stopped, going quiet. Andrew held his breath. A few moments went by and all remained silent. Andrew could almost feel the beast standing on the other side of the wall waiting and listening for him to make some type of noise. Despite the cold, sweat broke out on his brow. The floor creaked again, the sound moving away from his position.

Andrew exhaled slowly, relieved. The very next moment, like something out of a nightmare, the entire window shattered, glass clattering on the ground just five feet from where Andrew knelt. A Sasquatch growled, sticking its head out of the window glancing back and forth in the dark and snapping its teeth. Andrew shrunk back as a monstrous, clawed hand missed his head by inches. The beast sniffed several times before withdrawing back into the building. It walked off and began demolishing the inside of the store.

Andrew sighed, his hands trembling. He realized that there was nowhere safe. In the distance the echo of gunfire and a woman's scream gave even more evidence that the town was being destroyed. He smelled smoke in the air. Dismayed and still not able to comprehend the full extent of the destruction, Andrew scowled helplessly in the dark. The question "why" kept popping into his head. What caused them to do this? "They're monsters," he murmured. "They killed my daughter." Anger resurfaced and his face grew taut. He fought back his fatigue as he shivered and waited.

Behind him somewhere in the darkness, a child started crying. Andrew glimpsed back unable to see anything in the pitch black of the night. The child's cries grew louder. Andrew forced back the desire to yell, "Shut the hell up, you're giving us away." The child continued to sob. He decided with some anxiety that he could not sit by and not try to help. Pangs of guilt burrowed into his mind, scolding him for hiding. Marshalling whatever strength and resolve he had left, Andrew pushed himself up with the help of his cane. His legs ached from staying in one position for so long.

He lumbered in near blindness around to the back of the bar where dim, yellowish light brightened a couple windows helping to illuminate the area. Next to the shed stood a girl, no older than eight years old, crying, with pieces of leaves and grass in her messy red hair that hung to her shoulders. She shivered crossing her arms, dressed only in jeans and a t-shirt. She looked up at Andrew with wide scared eyes.

"My mommy needs help," she cried.

Andrew rushed over to her and kneeled down. "Shhhhhh. We have to be quiet. We can't let them hear us." The girl nodded and wiped her eyes, her cheeks streaked with tears. "Where's your mother?" Andrew asked in quiet whisper.

"The monsters took her," she said and began to cry. "Please help me find my mommy. The monsters came into our home. My mommy helped me out of my window and told me to run for help."

"Where do you live?" Andrew whispered, noticing the girl's red hair was the same color as Sherrie's.

"Down the road by the river." The girl turned and pointed behind her where a dark field of grass disappeared into the night.

"What's your name?" Andrew patted her shoulder and cringed when he looked at her hair again. He took his scarf and placed it around her neck.

"Casey," the girl whispered.

"Casey, my name is Andrew. I will take you back to your home and find your mother, but you have to promise me that you will be quiet. Those monsters are Sasquatch. We don't want them to find us. Will you promise to be quiet?"

Casey nodded. "Yes," she whispered. "Scout's honor."

"Good." Andrew hooked his cane to his belt, grabbed Casey's hand and in the other he clutched the handgun. They moved away from the back of the bar into a field of frozen grass and snow towards the Salmon River. "I hate kids," Andrew thought as he led Casey into the darkness. "Nothing but trouble." Despite his grumpiness, a strong overpowering feeling overwhelmed him that he would protect this child from harm with his life. He would not let anything happen to her. They had killed his daughter and her death still haunted him. If he had just reached Sherrie a few minutes earlier he could have saved her. "At least I killed it," he thought grimly. The Sasquatch that had murdered his daughter had been a massive, giant beast, most likely the leader of the group.

They hiked across the field, their pace slow, as they moved through the darkness. The shrill cries of the Sasquatch continued to pierce the night. He looked back and saw some of the buildings were on fire, crackling loudly. Up ahead, the sound of the Salmon River could be heard. They cut across the field towards a side street where a handful of houses stood, many with lights in the windows. Other houses were completely dark. Andrew wasn't sure if that was a good sign. Perhaps they were hiding. Fire engulfed one house, crackling flames shooting up from the roof with embers floating in the wind.

"Where's your home?" Andrew asked.

Casey pointed.

"The one on fire?" Andrew's said in a gentle tone.

She shook her head. "The one next to it."

The house next to the one engulfed in flames had lights on in most of the windows. They hurried across the field and as they got closer, Andrew noticed some of the windows on the houses were shattered, back doors ripped opened an entire section of a fence had been knocked down.

Andrew came to an abrupt halt and grimaced. The flames revealed a tall, shadowy shape emerging from between two of the houses, walking in front of the fire like some demonic beast. The Sasquatch gazed at the fire for a moment and then turned in their direction and stepped into the field. Andrew dropped to his knees and pulled Casey down. They lay down on their stomachs, much of the grass brittle and cracking underneath their weight. "Be quiet," Andrew murmured.

The heavy, crunching steps of the Sasquatch grew closer as the beast lumbered through the field. Casey went rigid, not moving a muscle. Andrew gripped her with one arm over her back as he hoped the grass and darkness would conceal them. The fire crackling over the house sent flickering shadows dancing faintly in the field. The Sasquatch stepped closer. Andrew clutched his gun praying he did not have to shoot. His gunfire would only attract more of the monsters like sharks to blood. The beast grunted making a throaty, spitting sound. It headed directly for their hiding spot, but veered away a few feet from them and walked by to the far side of the field, vanishing into the deep of the night, its footsteps fading away to nothing.

Andrew remained motionless as he felt Casey shivering next to him. He finally sat up, taking a quick glimpse behind him. "Let's go Casey," he whispered. They stood up and walked slowly across the field each of them tensing when a shrieking roar shot through the night like some barbaric war cry.

They reached the back of the houses where the destruction was even more visible. Fences were knocked down and in one yard lay the body of a dog that was twisted in a mutilated position, its head ripped off. Andrew blocked Casey's view so she would not witness the gruesome sight. They passed by two more dogs that must have fought to the death protecting their masters. One lay sprawled across a porch, dark blood dripping down the steps. They hurried past the burning house, the heat like a hot wave moving over them.

"That was Mr. Connor's home," Casey said. "He always came over and ate dinner with us."

"Shhhh," Andrew hissed sharply as they approached Casey's house. Embers had landed on the roof and one section had already caught fire, the flames were spreading quickly. A chain link fence lined the back yard, but one section had been ripped down, the metal bent and snapped off. They stepped through the hole to the back steps; one window was open.

"Is that where your mom helped you out?" Andrew whispered. Casey nodded, her eyes tearing again. Andrew patted her on the head. "You stay right here and don't move. I'm going to look inside for your mother. Remember to be quiet. I'll be right back."

Casey nodded as Andrew stepped up the cement steps and tried the back door. Surprisingly it was unlocked, so with gun raised, he opened the door and entered quietly. The smoke hung strong and putrid in the kitchen. Inside, the destruction of the attack was evident in every room with furniture overturned, glass shattered, holes punched in the walls. Andrew reached the living room where the front window was shattered, glass shards peppering the rug. The front door was on the floor, cracked in two pieces. The television had an enormous hole in the screen as if something had kicked it.

Andrew glanced in the kitchen but the smoke was too thick, the ceiling black with hot embers as if the flames were about to break through. He hustled down the hallway and found another door ripped off of its hinges. There was blood and clumps of blonde hair on the floor. Andrew grimaced, shaking his head. "I doubt she made it," he thought sadly as he opened the closet and found Casey's coat. He grabbed it and also a picture of Casey and her mother that was lying on the floor. He stuffed it in his coat pocket and returned to the hallway coughing, as the smoke grew thicker and fouler.

Andrew exited out the back door and to his surprise found Casey missing. He glanced about worriedly, his eyes adjusting to the dark. "Casey," he whispered as loud as he dared. "Casey," He fished out his flashlight and turned it on briefly scanning the back yard and the bushes. He turned if off and frowned. "Casey," he said in a louder voice.

Casey screamed somewhere near the field, the sound sending chills through Andrew's sore body. His face flashed with anger and creased with deadly seriousness as he rushed across the back yard towards the heart wrenching sound.

"I won't let you die," he yelled madly and readied his handgun.

CHAPTER 11

Stephen Denmin led his team, Victor, Henry and Tim, down the dark road towards Hyder. They walked in a line, flashlights shining around and glocks ready. He had called Bill, their helicopter pilot, who was at the hotel in Stewart. Bill reported that there had been sporadic attacks in Stewart as well, people panicking and gunfire could be heard. It would take Bill, who was spooked to hell, twenty minutes or more to drive to the small Stewart airport, refuel and fly the helicopter to pick them up. While they waited, Stephen decided to return to Hyder to find out what was happening. There was putrid smoke in the air and the roars of the Sasquatch could still be heard.

"Sure sounds like a hell of a lot of them up ahead," Stephen said with a determined grimace. His eyes gleamed with excitement as the opportunity of revenge had finally arrived after all these years.

"We need to capture at least one," Victor noted, his voice cracking with building fear. "I have my work to do."

"You will have one I guarantee it," Stephen huffed. "But most of them are going down. These bastards killed my wife and they are not getting away this time."

"Let's wait for the chopper. Getting myself killed wasn't part of the bargain," Victor quipped and slowed his pace.

Stephen glared at him. "It will be here soon enough. We have an opportunity here that we must seize. We need to get these Bigfoot before other people arrive. The police are going to close off the area by tomorrow, I'm sure of it. Reporters are going to be swarming the place like cockroaches and every so called Bigfoot expert will be here."

"Hey," Henry called out from behind, stopping abruptly, his beam of light halting at a clump of trees near the road. "I heard something."

A branch snapped in the vicinity and Victor fired at the trees without hesitation. The others followed blasting the area with their glocks. A few tense moments later, Henry signaled for them to cease. Branches and needles fell to the ground from their onslaught.

"Let's go," Stephen ordered. "If its out there, its dead. Nothing could withstand that kind of firepower." They continued their trek as Stephen tried calling Andrew again, but there was no answer. He dialed Chad and Alberto and received the same result.

The team rounded a bend in the road and found a lamppost knocked over, lying across the road. Farther down the road, there was more evidence of destruction with a car upside down, the windows splattered with what looked like blood. They approached the car, a black Oldsmobile, with caution. The headlights were still on and when they reached the vehicle, they saw the body. The shredded remains of clothing were around the corpse looking as if they had been ripped off. Five feet away lay a dismembered arm. The throat had been slashed and large swaths of flesh were missing with teeth marks on the bruised skin.

"They ate him," Stephen muttered in disgust. "The assholes ate him."

"Let's wait for the helicopter," Victor demanded. "This is bullcrap. We've already lost Greg."

"We don't know if he's dead," Henry cut in angrily. "We have to find him."

"We will when the helicopter gets here, now come on," Stephen snapped and walked off down the road away from the dead body. The others followed, while the smoke grew more pronounced in the air.

Something behind them growled, harsh and loud. Henry twirled and fired, but there was nothing to be seen, but the body and overturned car. They stopped in their tracks when deep grunting moved to their right in the black of the undergrowth.

"They're everywhere," Victor cried and started firing madly.

"Victor," Henry yelled. "Stop, you ass. Save your ammo."

Victor glared at Henry and lowered his gun. Without another word they walked around a corner in the road and reached the edge of town. Stephen halted, mouth agape with surprise. The sign post that read "Hyder Town Limits and "Entering Alaska" had been pushed down. The light post as well as wire cables were laying on the ground sending sparks of electricity into the air. Several houses were on fire, the snapping flames rising high, black smoke blotting out some of the stars.

Shock lined Stephen's face before anger flushed through his cheeks, his eyes turning into hard beads. These monsters had murdered his wife destroying his marriage of 27 years. He had hunted these creatures for the last four years and now they appear out of nowhere attacking this small town, killing who knows how many people, wives, husbands, sons, and daughters. It made him sick. He felt his whole body flare with energy and exhilaration preparing for action. This had been the day he had been waiting for and now it was upon him. They would pay for their crimes against humanity in blood. "A life for a life," he swore between clenched teeth.

In the distance, gunfire thundered somewhere in town and then a man yelled in desperation and terror before being silenced. Dark, hulking shapes raced quickly crossing the road disappearing between the houses.

Victor hurried over to an overturned car. "We have to get out of here Stephen. I didn't want to come out here in the first place. The fieldwork is for you to do. My place is back in the lab."

"Shut up," Stephen commanded. "There's nothing we can do about it now. Just keep your eyes open."

Tim walked to the side of the road flashing his light on the bushes that lined the front yard of a souvenir shop. He stopped as his eyes caught movement in the area of the bushes he had just passed. He flashed the light back and gasped. Black eyes were staring at him from within the leaves. The entire bush shook and burst forward as a nightmarish beast emerged lunging with amazing speed grappling Tim in an instant and lifting him up with little effort.

The others turned towards the ruckus, aghast, a seven foot Sasquatch stood in their midst. With a roar it flung Tim through the air slamming him hard against the side of the car. Tim collapsed to the ground motionless. Henry aimed his glock and blasted away at the beast that had already turned to flee back into the brush. He clipped it in the shoulder and back. The beast cried out stumbling into the dark.

Victor squatted next to the car, his eyes brimming with terror as he frantically glanced about like a hunted animal. Stephen rushed over to Tim and kneeled down finding his neck broken and blood oozing from his lifeless eyes.

"Holy damnation," Stephen cursed at the top of his lungs.

Henry charged into the bushes after the Sasquatch, yelling angrily. Stephen glanced about and stumbled over to Victor. With no warning, a three-foot log whizzed by Stephens's head and crashed into the car. At the same time, a tree cracked and shook back and forth in violent motions at the far side of the road before it fell towards them striking the ground only fifteen feet away.

Stephen shot his gun in the general direction unable to see any of his attackers. "Henry," he yelled, "Get your ass back here. Get up Victor and help us you little bastard."

Crouched next to the car Victor glared at Stephen, but finally relented and with much visible effort he stood up. With his quivering hands he fired his glock, his face white. Henry appeared pushing through the bushes sprinting over to them.

"It's dead. I killed the bastard. Is Tim..."

"Dead," Stephen said.

"Where the hell is the chopper?" Victor yelled in panic. "We need to call the second chopper too. We need reinforcements and it will take longer for the second one to reach us."

"Already have, but it will take several hours to get here."

Trees along the road began to shake; pine needles and branches dropped to the ground. Apish grunts broke out turning into shrill, high-pitched screams of rage that made each of them shake involuntarily. They had never heard such horrifying sounds.

Fear cracked Stephen's façade as he took a step back, startled at what he saw. At least a dozen Sasquatch stood in the tree line, dark, black shapes, staring at him, pronouncing him dead on sight. The trees shook furiously and a rock the size of soccer ball smashed into the road in front of their feet bouncing past them. Henry and Stephen yelled in defiance and fired at the Sasquatch that faded back into the undergrowth for cover. Victor cowered behind the car dialing Bill and telling him to get the helicopter here now. Another rock sailed through the air and bounced against the top of the car and nearly hit Victor who dropped down yelling.

"Help us," Stephen commanded harshly.

Victor blasted away with his gun when they heard a thundering crack and another tree toppled towards them. Stephen and Henry stumbled to the left trying to dodge out of the way as the tree crashed down, branches knocking them to the ground. Victor ducked behind the car, branches scratching and tearing into his clothes pinning him down.

The Sasquatch began to advance, a smaller one, six feet tall, thick and bulky, rushed forward leaping over the base of the tree in a single bound. It charged at them and if not for Henry's quick reaction they would have been killed. Lying on his stomach on the road, Henry fired his glock catching the beast in the stomach and chest as it leaped at them. The Sasquatch tumbled to the ground a few feet away, blood splattering across their faces. Stephen stood up and pulled a flare out of his jacket and fired at the tree line. A burst of bright flamed ignited, illuminating the area with blinding light revealing several Sasquatch who were caught by surprise shielding their eyes and retreating back into the shadows. Henry jumped up and shot a burst of gunfire at them. "We need to find cover."

"Well make our stand in the souvenir shop," Stephen said and shot another flare. He dropped the flare gun to the ground and clutched his glock. They ran around the car and found Victor climbing out from underneath thick branches his face scraped and bleeding.

"Come on," Stephen yelled running to the half collapsed porch of the souvenir shop. The others followed him through the front door that had been busted off its hinges. As the bright lights of the flares diminished, the Sasquatch began to advance again on the building ready for the kill.

CHAPTER 12

With an urgent overwhelming sense of purpose, Andrew rushed across the back yard towards Casey's screams. He passed through the hole in the chain-link fence; gun in hand as he leaned heavily on his cane. There was no way in hell he would let any harm come to Casey. He swore this girl would survive this invasion. Sherrie had died waiting for him to come and rescue her. He had failed miserably reaching her too late. The image of Sherrie's broken body lying on the forest floor would forevermore haunt his mind. He would not fail. "Not this time," he muttered as anger creased his face.

Outside the fence, to his left, the house burned in a conflagration of flames and smoke billowing up in the air. His shadow danced on the ground in front of him, fading into the dark field. He rushed passed the flames as heated air blew by him. Casey charged into sight from between the burning house, bolting into the field.

"Casey," Andrew yelled.

An instant later, a Sasquatch barreled through a wood fence, smashing the entire structure down. He caught sight of the girl and chased after her. Andrew aimed his handgun and pulled the trigger, gunfire thundering. The bullet struck the beast in the arm and it stumbled and fell to the ground. Casey ran towards him, but he had already forgotten about her as his face twisted with rising anger. Andrew crunched over the frozen grass of the field towards the Sasquatch intent on killing it. "You killed my daughter, you freak of nature," he whispered and let off another shot. The beast growled, jumped up and charged. Andrew stopped, surprised by its swift recovery and ferocity.

"You killed my daughter," Andrew bellowed at the top of his lungs, eyes bulging with an ire bordering on madness. He shot again and again yelling and cursing until finally the Sasquatch collapsed ten feet away. Andrew approached it cautiously and aimed for the head. He pulled the trigger, blood and brains splattering. He holstered his gun and began pounding the corpse with his cane slamming the silver handle into its back.

"You ruined my life," Andrew yelled hoarsely and smacked the corpse again. "You were a lie to me. I thought you were creatures of peace."

SMACK

"You were nothing of the sort."

SMACK

"Monsters… murderous creatures of hell," Andrew shrieked, his voice harsh and dry.

SMACK

"I wasted my life trying to learn more about you when I should have spent the decades hunting each and everyone of you demons down and wiping your existence from the face of the earth."

SMACK

"Did you find my mommy?" Casey asked from behind him.

Incognizant of her presence and not hearing a word, Andrew's face reddened with unbridled rage as he raised his cane over his head. His entire focus was on the bloodied corpse below him. He struck with a vengeance.

SMACK

"I swear to you and your kind that you have made an enemy. I pledge my life to seeing your destruction."

SMACK

"You made a fatal mistake when you killed my daughter. Sherrie meant you no harm. She was here for peace, to learn about your kind, to protect you, to communicate with you and what did you do… You killed her." His entire face flushed with rage, blood vessels raised, eyes crazed and unseeing. With a loud yell he struck again.

SMACK

"Andrew," Casey said keeping her distance. "Did you find my mommy?"

Andrew raised his cane again and hesitated. Casey's voice registered somewhere in the maelstrom of his mind. Several seconds passed before he lowered his cane and took several deep breaths, exhausted from the emotional display. He turned in weariness towards Casey, his face bereft of anger, replaced by a sullen, heavy weight. He looked at the scared little girl for a moment and shook his head.

"Your mother wasn't there," Andrew pronounced sadly and walked over to her, each step taking much effort. He handed Casey her coat and wiped the handle of his bloody cane on the grass.

"Where is she?" Casey cried as she put on the coat.

"I don't know Casey... hopefully hiding somewhere."

Part of the burning house collapsed with a loud crashing and crackling sound. They turned to see Casey's house was now entirely consumed in flames. Nearby, a Sasquatch screamed a loud, freakish war cry that was becoming too familiar.

"We have to leave here Casey. It's not safe." Andrew took her hand and they walked away from the burning houses, back into the cover of darkness in the field towards the Salmon River. He wanted to get as far away as possible from any building where the Sasquatch were swarming. "Where the meat is," he thought in disgust.

They approached the Salmon River and came to an eight-foot tall chain link fence. "Do you know where the gate is?" Andrew whispered, unable to see much in the dark.

"Yes," Casey said. "I play by the river all the time. My mom took me fishing last summer." She led them about twenty yards to the right and opened a gate. The ground sloped down and they stepped cautiously. White clouds covered much of the sky, but in the openings, the brightest stars, numberless, shined overhead. "A night sky brimming with stars," Andrew thought randomly. He remembered Chad telling him that in Los Angeles, there were maybe three or four stars in the night sky.

The Salmon River grew loud and Andrew could make out its dark surface ahead of them. The ground dropped off down the bank. Andrew climbed down and was about to help Casey, but she scaled the bank quickly with little effort.

A Sasquatch roared, deep and powerful, echoing across the river.

"That sounded close," Andrew whispered. "Where can we hide?"

"This way." Casey grabbed Andrew's hand and pulled him along the lower bank. There were many rocks and slick logs and roots that they had to navigate around and climb over. They reached a side of the bank that dropped down four feet. The thick, overhanging vegetation created an alcove. They moved into the darkness of the hideaway and sat down next to each other, their backs against the cold dirt wall.

"This is my secret base," Casey said. "I come here to hide sometimes when we play hide and seek. My friends never find me."

"This is perfect," Andrew whispered, his thoughts returning to the Sasquatch. He pulled out his cell phone and noticed that Stephen had tried calling him again. He dialed him back, but Stephen did not answer. He called Chad and Alberto only to get their voice mail. "Where are you guys?" he whispered.

"Are you calling for help?" Casey asked. "There's no police in Hyder."

"A damn shame," Andrew muttered. "I'm trying to call my friends to see if they are all right."

"I'm sorry about your daughter," Casey said.

"What?" Andrew asked, shocked.

"I heard you say the monsters killed your daughter."

Andrew nodded. "They did," he murmured, his throat constricting with grief.

"Why did the monsters come here?" Casey asked. "We didn't do anything bad."

Andrew gave her a hug. "I wish I knew and I promise you I will find out. Those monsters aren't going to get away this time. They've crossed a line. I promise I will help you find your mother."

"Thank you," Casey said warmly.

Both of them grew quiet listening to the sound of the Salmon River flow by them. Occasionally they would hear a nightmarish cry, but it was usually in the distance. Although Andrew's anger had diminished from exhaustion, he felt some satisfaction in killing the Sasquatch and beating it with his cane. It had been an emotional outlet he needed. He had kept much of his emotions, dealing with his daughter's death, bottled up and all of it had broken loose at once. It had felt good to release it instead of trying to banish it with martinis. He had purged much of the helplessness, regret and guilt from his system, but the ire would not leave.

"I don't want it to leave," he thought darkly. "They killed my daughter and nothing will ever change that fact."

Andrew wondered if Stewart had been attacked also, guessing dozens of Sasquatch, maybe close to a hundred had been involved with the invasion tonight. "A very scary thought." These

Sasquatch were the ones that had attacked Camp Elizabeth where the nightmare had started. He had not been at the camp during the massacre, but had gone up several times afterwards searching for them. And now they were here, four years later, doing same thing all over again.

"Chad and Alberto better be out of danger," Andrew thought. Alberto's family had gone through enough pain and heartache with the deaths of Enrique and Javier. He had no desire to be responsible for another death in that family.

Andrew rubbed his aching knees. Although he had a weathered face for being out in the elements all of his life, physically he was strong, easily able to compete with someone ten years younger, except for his bad knees. Some days they were fine and other days they ached with each step. He had spent a lot of money on knee surgery, but once they were damaged, they were never the same again.

"When will help come?" Casey asked in a tired voice.

"Not until daybreak I'm guessing. The monsters should be far from here by then."

"Good," Casey said and leaned her head against Andrew.

"It's going to be a long night," Andrew whispered staring out at the Salmon River as he put his arm around Casey to keep her warm.

CHAPTER 13

Chomping into the manthing's legs, the Scout tore a mouthful of flesh and chewed ecstatically. It had killed its victim with ease, breaking down the door and entering the house. The manthing had tried to fight back, but like all of these weak creatures, they were helpless before its might. The Scout had killed him within a few short seconds.

The Scout crouched down over the manthing in the living room as it listened to the victorious roars of its brothers outside. They had caught the manthings' dwelling by surprise, unaware of their impending doom, and had slaughtered them with little effort. The Scout did not want the night to end. It had waited too long to strike back at its enemies who were like ants, numberless and always spreading out. It wanted to savor this victory for as long as possible. The Scout hoped that they could attack more often, regretting that they had not done this sooner.

Stabbing its hand deep into the stomach of its victim, it took out a handful of innards and stuffed them in its mouth. It had been a long time since the Scout had fed on so much, most nights going hungry.

With sudden alertness, the Scout glanced up, its black eyes narrowing. It had heard a quiet thump nearby. It listened, but the sound did not repeat. It started sniffing, catching another scent. The Scout stood up, its thick muscles tensing, blood dripping from its sharp claws. It stepped across the floor, the wood groaning under its great weight. It walked up the stairs to the second level of the house, some of the steps cracking.

The Scout moved down the hallway that was nearly too narrow for its wide body. It approached a closed door to its left and with one forceful strike from its fist, knocked it off of its hinges. A faint, startled cry came from within the room. The Scout growled and entered walking over to the bed and flipping it over sending it slamming against the wall. To its disappointment, no one was hiding underneath.

Rage burned through its face. It rushed over to the closet door and stabbed its claws into the wood tearing the whole structure off the wall. A female manthing screamed from within the closet. The Scout's mouth watered with anticipation as it stood in front of the closet enjoying the moment. It growled and the female screamed again like some terrorized animal knowing that death was near.

The Scout reached into the space, seized the female's leg and pulled her out as she screamed and flailed her limbs. It raised her in the air upside down and shook her violently. The female kicked and ripped hair from its legs with her hands. It growled and with one mighty swing, the Scout flung her against the wall, silencing her. Grabbing the manthing by the ankle, it dragged her out of the room and back down the stairs where the half eaten corpse of the male lay on the bloody floor.

Letting go of the female for a moment, the Scout kneeled down and finished its meal. Satisfied, it stood up and dragged the female out of the house where several of its brothers were lumbering along the street. Many of them were dragging bodies of their own or carrying them over their shoulders. Some of their captives were still alive, crying, struggling to break free or screaming. The smell of smoke lay thick in the air and many of the manthings houses were on fire. Satisfaction filled the Scout's eyes before a sense of urgency descended upon it.

The Scout knew it was time to leave. Countless manthings would come swarming over the area shortly. They would bring their fire weapons and flying metal birds. The manthings could travel great distances through the air. They would search for them scouring the forest. The Scout had to be faster and smarter than the manthings.

The Scout raised its head up at the night sky and gave a high-pitched punctuated scream in quick timed bursts. The others nearby looked in its direction and proceeded to do the same, making the exact scream spreading the signal.

Sasquatch began appearing on the road, emerging from the houses, out from behind buildings, most of the carrying bodies. The signal continued to spread through the town until the whole night sky echoed under the haunting scream

The Scout dragged the female and walked quickly, its heavy footsteps crunching in the snow. It moved north out of town back into the forest. Others joined it, all of them growing silent as they disappeared into the dark.

CHAPTER 14

Stephen and Henry finished barricading the entrance to the souvenir shop with a cabinet, a couple chairs and whatever else they could find. The shrieks and growls of the Sasquatch increased into a mad frenzy sending chills through everyone in the room. They backed up to the center where Victor cowered behind a counter.

"Don't panic," Stephen yelled. "We have guns, bullets and brains. They can't stand against our gunfire. Don't let those animals win." He looked towards the door and aimed his glock steadying his trembling hand. "Don't waist your ammo."

Henry locked the back door and returned to the group. "We should be…" Henry started to say when the window next to him shattered inwards; a monstrous, dark hand reached in swiping at him with knife-like claws. Henry jumped back and blasted the window with his glock. The Sasquatch cried out and withdrew.

A loud thump hit the roof above them followed by another and another. The ceiling creaked and the sounds of several Sasquatch scrambling over the top of the store could be heard. Victor pointed his gun at the ceiling and fired.

"No, Victor," Stephen snapped. "Save your damn bullets for shots that will count."

Footsteps thumped against the roof as bits of the ceiling flaked down upon them. Stephen grew angrier, his fierce eyes narrowed and his brow creased with disdain. This mission was not turning out as planned. They were supposed to be on the offensive, hunting those bastards deep in the forest. Instead they were cowering in a wrecked souvenir shop fighting for their lives. "They're just dumb animals," he thought. "What the hell is going on? This won't happen again. If I have to buy myself an army to wipe these monsters out, I will."

The make shift barricade that blocked the ruined remains of the front door burst inwards in one sudden attack, sending debris flying as a Sasquatch barreled through and charged right at them. Victor fell back screaming. Stephen aimed his glock and fired, his shot went awry as a piece of wood clipped his arm. Henry dropped to his knees and shot his glock striking the beast with several bullets. The Sasquatch swung its long arms at Henry who leaped to the left, falling down. Grabbing its stomach, blood oozing though its hairy fingers, the Sasquatch stumbled backwards out of the front door.

The walls of the shop began to shake and the few items still on the shelves crashed to the floor. A long crack formed along one of the walls and buckled inwards.

"They're trying to knock the whole building down," Stephen yelled wishing he had brought some of the explosive devices. Henry crept up to the window, stuck his glock through and began firing. A Sasquatch cried out and backed off. A second wall cracked down the center, the paint chipping off.

"Don't panic," Stephen snapped. "We will get out of this." He shot through the front door as a Sasquatch rushed up onto the porch. Victor finally managed to get some courage and blasted his glock. The crack grew wider on the wall and a hairy fist punched through and withdrew to ram it again.

Over all of the commotion, they heard a sudden, loud shrill scream punctuated in quick bursts. This cry was repeated as another Sasquatch joined in, followed by another and another until all of them were making that haunted noise.

"What the hell are they doing?" Stephen asked, baffled by the sound.

"They're going to rush us," Victor cried.

The walls stopped shaking and then the eerie screams stopped all at once. The growling and roaring ended and everything went unnervingly still. Stephen, Victor and Henry stood in the middle of the ruined store glancing at each other questioningly. All of them were breathing hard, hands trembling. They expected the assault to start again, but all remained quiet.

Stephen motioned for them to stay where they were, then he walked slowly to the front door, his steps crunching over broken glass. He moved cautiously, his glock raised, and his finger on the trigger. He climbed over a fallen cabinet and reached the black, gaping entrance where the door once stood. He peered out for a moment and then stepped out onto the half collapsed porch.

"Did they leave?" Victor blurted.

Stephen stepped back in and shrugged his shoulders. "Looks that way."

"Where did they go?" Henry asked and walked out onto the porch to take a look for himself. Outside, the only evidence of the

Sasquatch was the destruction that they had left behind: trees were lying across the road; cars were overturned; a fire was spreading quickly burning a house next door. "They vanished just like that." Henry shook his head in disbelief. "I thought they had us near the end. I always wondered how thirty hunters at Camp Elizabeth, who had weapons, were so easily killed by these creatures. Part of me always thought they must have been pussies. Gosh, those things are ferocious and strong. I shot one a couple times and it kept coming."

Stephen called the helicopter pilot Bill on his cell, spoke for a minute and hung up. "He says it will be another twenty minutes before he gets here, said there were a few attacks on the outskirts of Stewart. It took him a while to reach the airport. He's refueling right now."

"Let's take the chopper and get the hell out of here," Victor said. "We can come back with a lot more men."

"No," Stephen shook his head. "This is our chance. They're on the run and we have to find them before they disappear for another four years. Bill is bringing explosives, more ammo and automatic weapons. We'll be fine. Once the authorities get here, they'll take over. We have to find these bastards before anyone else. We won't get caught by surprise."

"At least wait for the second helicopter so we'll have more men," Victor protested.

"The second chopper won't get here for at least an hour and by then it will already be too late."

"Plus we still have to find Greg. He may still be alive," Henry said.

"Agreed." Stephen nodded. "Those bastards took many of the hunters at Camp Elizabeth to their lair. By the time the authorities found the cave, all that was left were skeletons. Those monster ate them."

"Those things are hideous. I hope Greg is okay." Henry shook his head in utter disgust.

Stephen sighed and spit on the porch. "You know they never found the body of my wife. Just thinking of those bastards attacking our cabin and dragging her off into the woods never to be seen again makes me so damn angry. I hope she didn't suffer."

"We'll make them pay." Henry patted Stephen on the shoulder.

"We will," Stephen muttered. "We will." He thought of his son and daughter and the fact that the same monsters that had murdered his wife had almost killed him. He had set up trust funds for both of them in case something happened to him. They would be set for life. It made him feel better since he had dismantled most of his company, selling much of the assets to fund his Sasquatch hunt. He was destroying the family business to kill these monsters. He had always thought his son and daughter would eventually work for the company, but things changed. "That's life," he thought. "No matter." Both of his children had graduated from college and were doing well.

Stephen had spent millions acquiring Victor's biotech company funneling much of the money into a secret project. Victor promised results and now that they were close to acquiring specimens, he was sure of success. Victor could be a pain and seemed lost in his own world much of the time, but the man was smart and on the same page as Stephen when it came to the Sasquatch.

Part of him hoped that these beasts would lead him to his wife's body. It had infuriated him that her body had never been found. There had been no closure, just questions that needed to be answered. He wanted to bring his wife home and give her a proper burial.

The Sasquatch had sent his life into an entirely different course than the one he had followed most of his life. They had been a thorn in his gut; a disruption that he could not control and he hated that helpless feeling. He had always been in control, running a successful mining company, making profits, hiring and firing.

"And these bastards attacked me tonight. How dare they," he thought. They have done enough harm. He had been forced on to the defensive.

"Not anymore," he thought. "The tide is about to turn." He would go on the attack and never be caught by surprise again. These monsters were not going to escape this time. He would hunt them to the ends of the earth. "You're mine," he promised as he heard the hum of the helicopter approaching their location.

"Bill's here," Stephen said walking out onto the road watching as the helicopter appeared over the treetops.

CHAPTER 15

Andrew flinched, startled when his cell phone rang sounding uncomfortably loud in the quiet of the night. He had been lost in thought sitting next to Casey in the darkness of the alcove listening to the sound of the Salmon River flowing by them. He thought he had silenced the ringer. Casey squeezed his arm and looked up at him. The name Stephen flashed on the cell phone.

"Stephen, Where are you?" Andrew asked.

"In the chopper. We were attacked outside of Hyder. Tim is dead and Greg is missing. A whole hell of a lot of Sasquatch attacked us and the entire town."

"Are Chad and Alberto with you?" Andrew asked.

"No, we haven't heard from them. No one answers their damn cell phones. Sheesh, from up here it looks like half the town is on fire. The Sasquatch made some weird screams all at once and vanished. We're going to hunt them down. It will be easy to follow them with the infrared cameras."

"I heard the screams too. Have they really left town?"

"Looks like it. Where are you? Time is a wasting. We'll pick you up and hunt these bastards down."

"I'm near the Salmon River. You go on without me. I'm with a little girl who lost her mother. I'm going to keep her safe until the police lock this place down. I also have to find Chad and Alberto. I'm worried about them."

"Ok," Stephen yelled over the blare of the helicopter. "I can't believe you're passing up this chance."

"Things change Stephen. Keep me updated and stay safe. We've lost enough people tonight."

"Will do," Stephen said and hung up.

"Is help coming?" Casey asked.

"My friends are going to hunt down those damn monsters so something like this will never happen again."

"Good," Casey whispered. "I want to find my mommy."

"We shall," Andrew promised. "My friends said that the monsters left town so let's go look for your mother."

Andrew stood up debating on whether he dare turn on the flashlight. He decided against it, since there was a high probability that there were lingering Sasquatch around. They climbed up the bank and walked along the chain link fence to the gate. All was quiet except for the distant sound of crackling fires. They trekked across the field towards Casey's home, which was completely in flames and had caught the house next to it on fire so three houses in a row were burning like bright torches. They moved out from the back of the houses to the front of the neighborhood street staying in the middle of the gravel road. A telephone rang in one of the houses whose front door was smashed open and the windows shattered but there was no sign of people. The phone kept ringing and finally stopped.

An overturned truck rested upside down in one of the driveways giving only a glimpse of the destruction. Andrew halted upon seeing a dark shape lying in the middle of the road. His curiosity got the best of him and he decided it was safe enough to turn on his flashlight. The illumination revealed a gruesome sight causing Casey to cry out. A dog, a boxer, had been ripped in two pieces; entrails and blood covered the road. Andrew steered clear of the corpse and walked up the street towards the main road.

In front of them, several buildings were in flames, a yellow light illuminating the night sky. Shots of gunfire boomed in the distance. Casey gripped Andrew's hand. He responded by shaking it lightly, signaling that everything would be ok.

Andrew's thoughts turned to Chad and Alberto as a worried feeling descended upon him. They were probably safe, hiding somewhere, he assured himself. Chad had survived two encounters with the Sasquatch. Andrew dialed their numbers again and grimaced when they went to voicemail. Alberto, on the other hand, he worried about even more, since he was new to all this and did not have Chad's experience.

They reached the main road and found it dark; all of the street lamps had been knocked down. Besides the yellowish light from burning houses, the only illumination came from a few windows. The wind blew, trees creaking as they swayed. The town looked empty, destroyed, isolated by the dark hills that rose up around it. Andrew coughed and rubbed his nose. The smoke was strong and stinging his eyes.

There were no signs of any people as they walked past ruined houses and smashed cars. Andrew was headed back to the bar when sudden movement caught his eyes as something darted between two houses. Casey screamed and Andrew flinched back and nearly dropped the flashlight. A dog raced past them barking.

"Whew!" Andrew sighed, blowing out a long breath. Casey smiled.

They reached the front of the bar where the door had been ripped out like most of the houses and buildings that they had seen. Andrew motioned for Casey to wait on the porch while he went to investigate. Disappointment lined his face when he found the room exactly how he left it, demolished with streaks of blood on the floor. He had hoped to find someone living, who happened to return after the destruction. The place was empty so he returned to the porch and took Casey's hand continuing down the road.

"Where's everyone?" Casey asked as they circled around another overturned truck with its wheels pulled off.

"Dead," Andrew snapped a little too harshly. "Like every damn person in this town."

Casey tensed.

Andrew realized what he had just said and tried to rectify the matter. "I'm sure some folks are alive hiding out until help arrives."

Ahead of them, the two-story general store burned and crackled in a conflagration of flames, embers floating through the air and black smoke billowing up into the night sky. Andrew had eaten lunch there several times with Chad at the sub shop on the second level. He remembered some friendly old lady was always at the cash register, but he could not remember her name. They veered to the far side of the road, the heat from the fire too strong. Casey coughed from the putrid smoke as they quickly passed by the store.

Andrew hastened his pace as an uncomfortable, foreboding feeling engulfed him. Had all the Sasquatch vacated the town or were a few lingering around waiting. They were quick and masters of ambush. Concern lined his eyes as he thought of the safety of Casey. He would not let anything happen to her. He just hoped he was quick enough to shoot if one suddenly jumped at them from behind a bush.

They approached the inn where Andrew, Chad and Alberto had been staying, thankful to find it still standing and not on fire. On closer inspection, the inn did not escape the destruction unscathed. Every door had been ripped off its hinges and each window had been shattered. A gaping hole stood in the wall next to the office, which was in complete shambles with blood splattered on the smashed front desk. Andrew tried to shield Casey from the blood. She had been through enough that night and did not need to witness any more horror.

Andrew walked along the side of the inn to his room. He turned the light on and found the table with his computer and notepads smashed in two, everything scattered on the floor. The room was not too badly damaged compared to some of the other rooms.

"Probably because I wasn't here, so they moved on to the next room to find their prey," he thought in dismay. They walked to Chad's room and Andrew peered in with some hesitation, sighing when he found it empty. "There's still hope that he is alive," he thought.

They moved to Alberto's room, where the lights were off, the bed overturned and the mattress shredded. The bathroom door was busted opened still hanging by one hinge. His eyes were drawn to the closet door, which was shut. He opened it and shined his flashlight. Alberto's wide eyes were staring back at him in terror.

"Alberto," Andrew exclaimed with surprise and grabbed his shoulder. The young Latino flinched, his eyes still wide, not focusing on anything, his body trembling in shock.

"Alberto," Andrew shook him forcefully. "It's me, Andrew."

Alberto's eyes slowly focused on Andrew and blinked. He began breathing deeper and faster. "Are they gone?" Alberto whispered.

"Yes, you have nothing to worry about."

"Are you sure?" Alberto noticed Casey for the first time and her presence seemed to give him more confidence. He crawled out of the closet and stood up. "Where did they go?"

Andrew shook his head. "They left all at once... made some strange screaming sounds, I'm guessing was a signal for them to depart."

Alberto nodded understanding filling his eyes. "I heard it to. They were attacking the inn, people were screaming, growling was coming from every direction. I hid in the closet and heard them enter my room, their steps were so loud shaking the entire floor. The footsteps were getting closer to the closet. I thought I was going to die and then they made that ghastly cry and the footsteps moved away and all went silent. I didn't dare leave the closet thinking one was waiting to kill me."

"Where's Chad? Have you seen Chad?" Andrew asked disturbed that there was no sign of his friend.

Alberto shook his head. "I haven't heard from anyone. He was going to the bar to see you. I turned my cell phone off not wanting it to ring and give away my hiding place."

"Chad left the bar shortly before the attack. He said he was going back to the inn," Andrew mused.

"He never came back." Fear filled Alberto's face.

Andrew grimaced and gazed out into the night.

CHAPTER 16

Stephen glimpsed out the window of the helicopter down at the dark treetops of the forest below him. He mumbled a curse word and returned his attention to the screen finding no heat traces with the infrared cameras. They had been circling around the south end of town near the barricade of trees attempting to spot a Sasquatch.

"Where the hell are they?" Stephen yelled in a burst of emotion. "There is no way on this earth that they are getting away."

"Let's try the north end. That's where Andrew was attacked," Henry said from the back seat of the helicopter. Victor sat next to him exhausted, a perpetual scowl on his face. Bill piloted the helicopter while glancing nervously at the others, obviously spooked from the attacks.

"Let's do it," Stephen motioned for Bill to head north. They flew over town passing by the fires that were engulfing many of the houses, black smoke billowing into the night sky. The infrared screen grew bright, reddish orange detecting the fires. Once they flew over the north end of town, the screen turned black. The helicopter dropped to just above the treetops, zooming back and forth in a methodical manner to cover as much ground as possible. An occasional heat trace from a bird perched on a branch or a scouring rodent made an orange dot on the screen, but no sign of Bigfoot.

"They couldn't have disappeared." Stephen pounded his fist on the equipment. "There were dozens of those damn things."

Victor leaned forward. "The Sasquatch are not going to be around this area. They left once they made that retreat call. If we're going to find them, we need to fly away from the town's perimeter. They move fast. I say go north and follow the road. There are a lot of hills and large stretches of wilderness. We need to capture one of them alive. We have a lot of money riding on this."

"Go north," Stephen commanded then turning to Victor. "Why so brave all of a sudden? You've been cowering back there all night."

Victor frowned, his eyes turning to ice. "I'm starting to get over the initial shock. They caught us by surprise. We came up here on a mission and I want it accomplished to our satisfaction. I have a lot of work to complete and it can not proceed until I have a live specimen."

The helicopter flew north staying near the road, occasionally passing over a house. About twenty minutes later, an orange blip appeared on the screen for only a few seconds before they passed by that swath of land.

"Wait," Stephen said. "We got something, fly back around."

The helicopter circled back and hovered in the area. The orange blip reappeared on the screen.

"Drop down some more," Stephen yelled excitedly.

As the helicopter descended the image became clearer until they could make out a humanoid shape squatting down near a tree gazing up at them, its clawed hands clasping the bark. Henry opened the door and aimed a tranquilizer rifle. He fired in the general direction and missed.

"Too many branches in the way," Henry yelled.

With sudden speed, the Bigfoot stood up and ran, vanishing from the screen. The helicopter followed, recapturing it as a moving orange blip.

"Damn they're fast," Bill said keeping the helicopter as low to the tops of the trees as he could.

The Bigfoot raced down a slope onto flatter ground where several more orange blips appeared on the screen all at once, laying and kneeling in the undergrowth. A screeching scream filled the sky loud enough that it could be heard over the whirl of the helicopter. The Bigfoot they had been pursuing raised its head and roared. All at once, the other Sasquatch rose from their hiding places and began sprinting in the same direction through the woods attempting to escape.

"They must know we can see them," Victor said.

"No escaping this time." Stephen smiled smugly.

The Sasquatch emerged from a line of trees, crossing a stream where their cameras caught more details of them. They reached the other side, leaping up the banks and disappeared back into the trees, moving along the base of a hill.

Henry put the tranquilizer gun down and picked up a rifle. He opened the door and fired blindly into the dark. The Sasquatch made jerking movements, startled by the gunfire. They bolted even faster through the woods.

Stephen laughed. "That scared the crap out of them."

The Bigfoot moved away from the base of the hill, around one side of a lake and made a sharp turn towards another hill that rose high into the night sky, a black looming shadow ahead of them.

Stephen watched the screen with a smug look of satisfaction, his fingers tapping rhythmically on his leg. He had these monsters in his sights and there was no way that they would escape. He had turned the tables on them and now he was the hunter again. Tonight he would have his revenge on these bastards for the death of his wife. He had never been the best husband, spending much of his time away on business with occasional one-night stands, but he had been a provider. A sense of guilt touched him for his unfaithfulness and for the fact that he had left his wife alone at their cabin to attend an emergency meeting. Why had he not asked her to go along? If he had she would still be alive and his life would be completely different. The guilt sometimes was too much, one reason he drank and kept himself busy, focused on work. He clenched his jaw promising that Claire would be avenged and his guilt would be put to rest.

"Stephen," Bill said. "I'm going to have to turn the lights on for a moment and get our bearings. We're coming up close to a cliff face and I don't want to hit it."

"Ok." Stephen nodded and flipped the infrared cameras off. The lights were turned on revealing a fast approaching rock wall. Bill pulled back on the steering stick bringing the helicopter to a stand still.

"That was close." Bill shook his head and let out a long sigh of relief.

"Turn the lights off," Stephen said with an impatient tone.

Bill complied and when the infrared cameras were switched back on, the screen came up black.

"What?" Stephen cried. "Where are they?" The helicopter flew along the side of the cliff and no heat impressions appeared. "They can't move that fast. We couldn't have lost them."

Victor stuck his head up front. "Turn on the spotlight. They must be hiding along the wall.

The spotlight flashed on revealing heavy undergrowth of brush and bramble growing along the base of the cliff face. The light stopped on what looked like the top of a cave entrance hidden behind tall bushes and other foliage.

"That's it. That's it," Stephen yelled excitedly. "Put her down."

"Is it safe?" Bill asked.

"It won't be safe until those beasts are dead or captured. Ready your weapons." Stephen clicked the safety off on his glock. The helicopter landed in a clearing near the cave entrance. Henry was the first out of the helicopter ready with an automatic rifle and a flashlight. Victor followed with a glock and his own light. They all wore backpacks filled with weapons, ammo and equipment.

"Should I stay in the helicopter?" Bill asked.

Stephen shook his head. "No, you're coming with us. We need all the manpower we can get. The other helicopter is on the way, but it will take awhile for them to reach us, so we're on our own for now."

Bill and Stephen joined the others outside as they approached the cliff, a black shadowy wall that loomed overhead blotting out much of the sky. With stern faces, they walked with apprehension through brush and around the trees jumbled together near the rock wall. They shined the flashlights back and forth, but were unable to see the cave entrance from the ground level.

Henry took out a flare gun and fired straight up, the sky above growing bright, illuminating the entire area. He fired a second one. Everyone searched the perimeter as the flares created moving shadows that ran along the ground. Victor fired his glock towards the tree line and stopped when he realized it had just been a shadow. Henry pushed through the thick brush, the branches snapping as he passed. He disappeared from sight.

"I found it," Henry called back to the rest of the team.

The others pressed through the wall of bushes and found a ten foot black, gaping hole in the side of a rock wall. The vegetation near the entrance was trampled. A path led to the left along the cliff.

"They are intelligent," Victor mused. "They're smart enough to leave the vegetation in front of the cave untouched, keeping the entrance hidden while they follow a trail along the base of the wall to go in and out. Look here." Victor's light revealed several giant footprints in the dirt and ice along the trail. Torn pieces of clothing were dangling from some of the branches. "They brought a few of the towns people with them."

"Greg might be in there," Henry said. "We have to find him. Who knows what they're doing to those poor people."

"Alright everyone, flashlights off and night vision goggles on. We will have the advantage. They won't be able to see us, but we will damn well see them. Keep alert at all times. We know those bastards are fast and ruthless. We'll kill as many as we can and bring one back alive. We have bombs if things get dicey. Everyone will be getting a big bonus when all of this is done." Stephen flipped his flashlight off and the others followed sending the area into pitch-blackness. They put on the infrared goggles and the landscape became shades of ghostly gray.

"Ready men," Stephen said as he turned to face the cave.

"Let's do it," Henry took the lead. With weapons ready, the four men stepped into the entrance, darkness swallowing them.

CHAPTER 17

Stephen discovered that the cave was actually an old mine. There were rail tracks down the center, portions of which were buried in the ground. The tunnel looked like a wide, square hallway with wooden support beams along each side, many of them rotting, crumbling or cracked. Sections of the ceiling were depressed and appeared as if they were going to collapse. Everywhere, piles of dirt and rubble cluttered the passageway warning that the mine was on its death knell. As they walked deeper into the mountain, the stale air took a turn for the worse with a foul odor growing more putrid and evident.

"The stink of the Sasquatch," Stephen thought as he stepped around the spokes of a rotted wheel. Except for their own breathing and the crunch of their footsteps against the hard, rocky floor, the cave was eerily silent. Everyone moved with extreme caution, bodies tense and fear brooding in their eyes. The night vision goggles created a gray, other worldly view of the cave, as if they were descending into hell itself. They knew that somewhere ahead were dozens of murderous monsters. With fingers on their triggers, they walked at a slow, cautious pace. Giant footprints were pressed in the dirt all over the place.

"Heavy traffic," Stephen thought. "We have indeed found their hiding place."

The walls began to spread out creating a crude room where they came to a halt. Another tunnel, just an opening in the wall, wide enough for one person to walk through veered off to the left. On the right wall was a rectangular opening about four feet in height. Henry kneeled down and peered into the darkness.

"Looks like it keeps going. We'd have to crawl." Henry stood up and looked to Stephen for directions

"Let's follow the main tunnel," Stephen said and continued down the center of the passageway, sidestepping a hole in the ground. The others followed without a word. Henry hustled ahead of Stephen taking the lead. Large footprints dotted the ground assuring them that they had made the right decision and warning that they were getting closer to danger. The pathway arched to the right where they found the ceiling had collapsed with rock and dirt, blocking their way forward. Stephen frowned, shining his light around the pile trying to find an opening. Henry climbed up the pile near the left wall and moved around the side disappearing from sight.

"It's clear once you get past the mound," Henry called back. "Lots of footprints."

They proceeded past the collapsed area, the stink of the air growing more pronounced. Henry halted and pointed to the floor where there was a round circular hole with a rusty ladder going into the depths. There were bits of clothing on the tips of the ladder and blood staining the ground around. The footprints beyond the ladder were few.

"Looks like they went down in the hole," Henry said.

"They can climb ladders?" Victor murmured more to himself. "Interesting."

"It's not too far down. They could have dropped to the ground without using the ladder," Henry guessed.

"Let's do it. They can't be far. The stink is getting unbearable." Stephen raised his gun ready for battle.

"I'll go first." Henry climbed down the ladder, which creaked with each shift of his weight. Stephen went next followed by Victor and Bill. They found the tunnel below to be an actual cave with rough rocky sides, various widths and heights. Whoever mined the hill decades before had not dug out this portion. Maybe it had just been discovered when the mining outfit went out of business Stephen surmised.

The cave floor descended, the ceiling rising up 15 feet in the musty air. Henry stopped in his tracks, gasping in surprise. Up ahead three Sasquatch waited in the pitch black, motionless, ready to ambush them. They made no sound, waiting patiently for them to approach. Stephen stood next to Henry. If not for their night vision goggles they would have been caught by surprise, unaware. One Bigfoot leaned back into a cleft in the right wall; its clawed hand clutching a protrusion of rock, its head peering out in their direction was all that could be seen. Another Bigfoot waited behind a fallen rock to the left, hunched down near the floor, both hands gripping the stone ready to leap over at them. The third Bigfoot stood on all fours above to the left on a ledge ready to pounce down like a tiger.

Stephen shuddered at the sight realizing how close to death they had just come. The night vision made the Sasquatch look like ghostly, gray shapes in the black of the cave.

"I'll take the two on the left. You go for the one on the right," Henry whispered and began firing his automatic rifle. Stephen shot his glock in quick bursts missing at first, but the loud gunfire startled the Sasquatch and it stumbled out of its hideaway in the wall. Stephen peppered it with several bullets, the beast crying out and collapsing to the ground. Victor and Bill, who stood behind them, were unable to get a clear shot, so they kept glancing back making sure that they were not being ambushed from behind. Henry fired at the Bigfoot on the ledge striking it several times causing it to tumble and crash to the ground. The Sasquatch behind the boulder ducked down out of sight. Henry moved forward firing at the boulder. Stephen followed a step to his right blasting away. The Sasquatch cried out in freakish shrieks before it tried to flee. They shot it in the back and it tripped and fell. Henry rushed over and put a bullet in each Bigfoot making sure that they were dead.

"Well done boys, well done. I was about to crap my pants," Stephen said and kicked one of the Bigfoot in the head. "You bastards killed my Claire."

Victor kneeled down and removed a black container from his backpack that contained a syringe. He took several vials of blood, a few hair samples and a swab off the tongue and stored them in the container.

"Why don't we just try to take one of these dead ones back and get the hell out of here?" Bill asked. "This is way too dangerous."

"We have to find Greg. He may still be alive," Henry snapped angrily.

"We're killing these bastards. I've waited four years for this," Stephen fumed.

Bill shook his head frustrated. "I'm a helicopter pilot, not some damn soldier."

"I pay you good money, so shut the hell up. We've got work to do so let's do it." Stephen headed down the tunnel. The others followed, except for Bill who stood for a moment pondering if he should return to the surface. As the distance between him and the others grew, he panicked and rushed after them, spooked.

They continued descending into the cave, the unsettling silence returning, palpable and smothering as if the heavy blackness was encroaching on them with a malice of its own. They moved slowly watching out for the next ambush. It was unnerving as they approached the turns in the cave, all of them wondering if a Bigfoot was waiting for them on the other side.

The stench was awful and the night vision glasses made everything nearby an eerie gray. It was like walking through a nightmare; the walls seemed to be closing in on them. Bill kept glimpsing behind him, terror evident on his pale face, expecting a hairy hand to seize the back of his neck at any minute. Victor walked with more confidence then he had all night, his demeanor tense but no where close to the panic that had possessed him earlier. They turned a corner and found a Sasquatch peering from behind a bend in the cave waiting for them. It ducked behind the wall before they could shoot.

"Get ready boys," Stephen said. "They know we're coming."

Henry took the lead as they approached the bend with extreme caution and trepidation. He let off a couple warning shots, the gunfire booming loudly through the cave. He drew closer and came to a sudden halt, scanning the area ahead. He fired another warning shot and proceeded slowly. Five feet from the bend in the cave, he shot again and rushed forward firing around the corner.

"Clear," Henry yelled. Stephen walked around the corner followed by Victor. Bill hesitated a moment, his stomach growing queasy with worry. He wanted to return to his helicopter and fly up to the safety of the sky above the woods. No Bigfoot would be able to get him in the air. Why had he agreed to go down into the caves? The next instant, he heard a scraping sound behind him. He caught his breath, twirled around baffled when his entire field of his vision turned a bright gray through his night vision goggles. Surprise and confusion gripped him as he wondered why the goggles had turned from dark to light. He heard heavy breathing and felt warm air brush against the top of his head. His eyes adjusted to the brightness and grew wide as he slowly looked up. A Sasquatch was glaring down at him. It snarled and flashed its teeth as Bill cried out and began to raise his weapon. The growling Bigfoot launched forward and slammed him against the rock floor before he had time to shoot. The impact knocked him out cold as his gun went cluttering away into the dark.

With its sharp claws, the Sasquatch raised its hands and struck down stabbing and ripping chunks of flesh and bone from

Bill's corpse. Stuffing some of it into its mouth, the Sasquatch chomped loudly and stood up.

Gunfire exploded in the air and the Sasquatch stumbled back as it was struck in the arm, chest and stomach. Victor yelled and kept blasting away until the beast collapsed in a spray of blood. Henry moved past Victor and rushed over to Bill.

"He's dead," Henry yelled. "The damn thing got him."

A loud roar rumbled through the cave followed by several apish shrieks coming from both directions. Henry stood up glancing back and forth.

Stephen rounded the corner and replaced the clip in his glock. "Damn," he cursed but his voice was drowned out by the oncoming cries of their enemies.

CHAPTER 18

A car horn honked in the distance and kept blaring, growing nearer and louder. Casey, who was lying on a mattress on the floor, sat up, still covered with a blanket and crawled over to Andrew, who had been sitting on the other end. Her eyes were wide with fear. They had sought refuge in Andrew's room at the inn since it was the least demolished. To keep some of the cold air out, they had leaned the fallen door over the entranceway. After a dinner of sandwiches, chips and soda they had sat down to get some rest and wait for help. Casey had fallen asleep while Alberto sat in a chair nervously glancing at the door, unable to relax.

The honking wailed louder and a second horn joined the first in quick beeps. Andrew struggled to his feet, his body sore and his knee aching. He steadied himself with his cane and turned on his flashlight. "Come on." He motioned for the others to follow. "Help may have finally arrived."

Casey rushed over to Andrew and grabbed his hand. He gave her the flashlight to hold. Alberto followed behind, his face tense, looking to be on the verge of panic. They pushed the door down and walked to the front of the inn where two trucks with several people sitting in the truck bed with rifles and flashlights, drove towards them. The trucks stopped and a man called out asking if they were all right. They were from Stewart and had come as soon as possible to help.

Ernest, a big burly man with a thick Canadian accent, said, "Stewart was attacked. People are saying by Bigfoot. A few houses on the west side of town were broken into and several people are dead or missing. We got a lot of phone calls from people in Hyder that the same thing was happening to them and then all the calls stopped. We tried contacting our friends and family but no one in Hyder is answering. A bunch of us decided to go see what the heck is going on and help out. Ginger and Chuck at the customs building are dead and then we found a whole section of the forest knocked down blocking the road. It took us a while to drive around it and now this crap. Hyder in flames."

"Are the authorities coming?" Andrew asked

"Yes, yes. Some have landed at the airport and many more are on the way," Ernest said, staring down the empty street at the burning buildings with anger and sadness in his eyes. "Are those devils gone?"

Andrew nodded. "They've gone back in the woods. Some of my team are trying to track them in a helicopter."

"Geez... I can't believe this is happening. Where is everyone? The town looks vacant."

Andrew shrugged his shoulders. "You better start searching the area. There might be survivors still hiding somewhere."

"Will do," Ernest said and walked back to the truck. Some of the men climbed down and went on foot to cover more ground and go into the homes and shops that were not on fire. The two trucks drove slowly down the road into town honking their horns.

"I hope they find my mommy," Casey said.

"I hope so too." Andrew sighed, at a loss at what to do next, which for him was a rare occurrence. Chad was still unaccounted for and Stephen had called earlier with the coordinates to a cave that they believed the Sasquatch had entered. That was over an hour ago and he had not heard from Stephen since, which worried him.

"Let's go back to the room for now where it's a little bit warmer," Andrew said. He tried calling Chad, Stephen, Victor, Henry and Bill but no one answered. He called the second chopper and found that it was on its way.

"What are we going to do boss?" Alberto asked.

Andrew looked at Casey for a moment and back to Alberto. The attack was over and they had survived. His friends and teammates were missing and he had to get back to business. "We're going to take Casey to Stewart where it's safe. Is that okay with you?"

Casey nodded. "My best friend lives in Stewart. We go to school there. She's having a birthday party next week."

"Do you know where your friend lives?"

"Of course silly."

"Good, we will take you to your friend."

They walked back outside as one of the trucks returned with a handful of survivors. Unfortunately none were Casey's mother. Another car pulled into town and four U.S. police officers got out assuring everyone that more reinforcements were on the way. Many of the survivors were hurt or in a state of shock. The police organized the trucks to carry the survivors to the hospital in Stewart.

The eastern sky began to lighten from black to a gray as dawn approached. Andrew, Casey and Alberto hitched a ride on one of the trucks. Outside of town they reached the barricade where many men with trucks and construction equipment were clearing the road. Chainsaws were buzzing loudly. The two trucks maneuvered through a narrow pathway that had been cleared on one side of the road.

They reached the Canada Customs building and found a Canadian police car with lights flashing parked nearby. The windows of the building and the entire side of one wall had been smashed open. Black plastic was covering what looked like a body on the ground next to the building.

As they approached Stewart, Andrew found to his relief that the electricity was on as they passed street lamps that were throwing a yellowish light over the road. A few of the houses along the way had their doors knocked down. Some of the fences were flattened to the ground. A chain-linked fence had been twisted in two. Once they reached the few blocks, which made up the town of Stewart, the lights were on in all of the buildings. People were massed outside in groups; many men and women were holding rifles or handguns while others were crying, fearful or confused. Some were bringing food and coffee to people while others were asking what they could do to help. Andrew could not help but notice the scared looks on their faces.

Andrew's thoughts returned to the Sasquatch. What had caused such a change in behavior? They had never been so bold attacking an entire town. "Chad was right; they are monsters."

The trucks reached the hospital and there were several people waiting, ready to help the wounded.

"Casey, is your friend's house nearby?" Andrew asked.

"Just a couple blocks away. I hope they're okay."

"They should be. It looks like Hyder got the brunt of the attack."

They walked along the street passing many people, some in deep conversations wondering if they were going to be attacked next. Some wanted to leave town and flee to the south. Others were asking if they had seen a loved one or family member, while some had somber expressions, standing alone, looking out towards the dark edge of town as if expecting another attack.

Casey walked quickly, excitement in her voice. "We're almost there."

"This was some scary crap," Alberto said.

"It is." Andrew patted Alberto's shoulder. "You did a good job tonight hiding in the closet. You survived this encounter when many people were not so fortunate."

"Thanks," Alberto said. "I just keep thinking of my uncle and brother and what they must have felt when they were attacked."

"Your uncle Javier was a brave man. He tried saving my life. If it weren't for him, the mother would have had me for dinner. Your uncle stabbed it in the back. Unfortunately, there were other Sasquatch around. We did not have a chance. Your brother Enrique was also brave. He was the first one who went down into the Ape Caves with me. He volunteered. A very pleasant young man with a great sense of humor."

"I miss them," Alberto said.

Andrew patted his shoulder. "I do to."

"I hope Chad is okay," Alberto said.

Andrew remained silent, his face tightening as he forced back thoughts of his friend's possible demise.

They turned the corner and Casey's face gleamed with excitement. "There it is." She pointed and ran towards a house. On the porch, a man, a woman and a girl about Casey's age watched them approach.

"Casey," the girl yelled happily jumping off the porch and running towards her. They clung to each other and both started crying. The man and woman on the porch rushed over with concerned looks.

"Casey," the woman said. "Where's your mother?"

Casey ran to the woman and hugged her. "The monsters came and mom pushed me through the window. Andrew and I came back and my house was on fire. I don't know where she is."

Andrew and Alberto talked to them for a while. The family had been indoors when the attack began. Thankfully, the Sasquatch had not invaded this deep into Stewart, but they had heard the ferocious roars. Andrew assured them that the Sasquatch were gone for now. They promised to watch after Casey until her mother was found.

"Goodbye Casey," Andrew kneeled over and gave her a hug.

"Be careful," Casey said. "Please find my mommy."

Andrew nodded and waved to the others. Alberto followed Andrew down the street, both of them quiet. People anxiously rushed by while cars drove slowly along the streets. Dawn had broken and with the coming daylight the area did not look so frightening. It seemed like it all could have been a nightmare, except when you glanced in the direction of Hyder, smoke and haze filled the sky reminding him that it was not a dream.

"What now boss?" Alberto asked.

Andrew looked west past the smoke towards the mountains that towered along the horizon. "We find Chad."

CHAPTER 19

Growling reverberated deep in the Scout's throat as it reached the clearing and found the helicopter in front of the entrance to its lair. It halted and kneeled down, black eyes scanning the perimeter. There were no manthings about that it could detect, but how did they find the cave? Its hairy face screwed with vehemence at the realization that the manthings had intruded its hideaway. The Scout stayed at the edge of the clearing listening for any sounds of its enemy. The sun had risen above the eastern hills making it squint. Usually during the day, it rested in the safety and dark of the cave. It was not use to direct sunlight and rarely went out during the day hours unless the situation was desperate. Occasionally it had gone out in search of food.

The Scout had led its brothers to victory, destroying the manthing's town and taking their corpses into the cave to feast on. Most of its brothers had returned to the cave, but the Scout had remained outside watching for any signs of pursuit. It infuriated the Scout that the manthings had flown in the air like a bird, reaching the cave without its knowledge.

The Scout stepped out from the tree line and cautiously approached the manthings' flying machine, which looked like some giant insect. It had seen many of these flying things in the sky. They were loud and the Scout always had plenty of time to hide. It had never seen one so close and did not fear such an unnatural looking object. It was asleep or dead without the manthing sitting within it. The manthings strength originated from its machines and without them, they were weak, pathetic, and grossly inferior. The Scout knew what it had to do. It touched the door of the helicopter. It felt dead. It wasn't alive. The Scout began growling again, deep at first building to a roar and then it grabbed the bottom and flipped the helicopter over on its side. The Scout proceeded to smash, tear and bend, taking its rage out until it was satisfied that this flying machine was destroyed.

The Scout's black eyes shifted to the cave entrance. It took a step forward and then halted abruptly. Its brothers would be able to kill any manthing that entered their lair. The Scout crossed the clearing and returned to the tree line. If any manthings left the cave or if more came from the sky or through the forest, it would ambush them. The Scout moved into the undergrowth where the shadows were dark, disappearing into the trees.

CHAPTER 20

The roars of the Sasquatch were so loud and frightening that Stephen, Henry and Victor trembled at the power of such an overwhelming sound. They were standing in the black of the tunnel glancing back and forth in both direction through their night vision goggles for the inevitable gray almost ghostly shapes of the Bigfoot. The body of Bill lay a few feet away near the cave wall. Beyond his body was the hulking mass of the beast that had killed him.

"Should we head for the surface," Victor yelled, his voice hard to hear over the rumble of the monsters.

"We have guns, we're smart, we'll be all right," Stephen rasped.

"We still haven't located Greg," Henry added.

"Tell that to Bill," Victor yelled back.

The first Sasquatch rounded the bend, bursting into sight at full speed, charging down the tunnel towards them. Its glowing gray shape made an easy target with the night goggles. Both Henry and Stephen fired their glocks sending the Bigfoot crashing to the ground twenty feet from their location.

"Watch our backs Victor," Stephen yelled.

"Will do." Victor turned and gazed down the tunnel with frantic eyes. He kept glancing down at Bill's body finding a curious perversion in it. At that moment, a thought dawned in Victor's mind, his face growing into a hard scowl. His eyes narrowed and he tensed, cold detachment pushed his panic away. He glanced briefly at the others as a malicious smile tarnished his pale face.

At that moment, the growls and roars stopped all at once and a tension-filled silence settled over the cave. Stephen and Henry looked questioningly at each other.

"Maybe they gave up," Henry offered.

"I doubt that." Stephen reloaded. "They can't reach us here. They come down that tunnel and they'll be in open sight, no cover. We have the upper hand with those bastards. Once the other helicopter comes well have reinforcements and be able to hunt them all down. No escape from this cave. Each time I shoot one, I wonder if that's the one that killed my wife."

"We'll shoot all of them then you'll know for sure," Henry offered.

"Damn straight," Stephen said looking back at Victor. "Keep watch behind us Victor."

"I am," Victor said with a touch of hostility, a bemused expression filling his face. His eyes remained cold and emotionless as plans churned through his mind.

The cave remained quiet except for their breathing and shuffling about as they checked their weapons. Stephen stared with a confident, grim expression. Within his night vision, two glowing figures of the Sasquatch appeared in a flash, charging around the corner with boulders raised over their heads. The Bigfoot flung the rocks down the cave tunnel as Stephen and Henry began to fire. The first boulder smashed Henry's chest with such force it knocked him off his feet and slammed him to the rocky floor. The second boulder fell short and hit the ground catching Stephen's feet sending him head first to the cave floor.

Dazed, Henry moaned and began coughing up blood. He was pinned to the ground with the boulder leaning on top of him. As Stephen struggled to sit up, several fresh cuts and abrasions on his body began to bleed. He felt for his glock since the night vision goggles had been knocked to the side of his face and all was dark. The roars of the Sasquatch thundered through the cave as the two Bigfoot raced forward with claws outstretched ready to strike. Victor had stepped back several feet out of the way and nearly hit Henry who lay in front of his feet in obvious pain. Victor's hands were trembling and for a moment he froze in place as if not sure what to do next.

The Bigfoot were nearly upon them when Victor dropped back several more feet, raised the glock and blasted away. The first Bigfoot lunged on top of Henry and struck him with its claws. Henry yelled, helpless and pinned to the ground when the gunfire caught the Bigfoot mid section. The beast cried out and leaped at Victor who retreated two more steps firing the glock. The Bigfoot fell short, claws missing his face by only a couple inches. It collapsed in front of him. Victor grinned perversely and shot it a few more times.

Stephen was yelling and cursing as he fought for his life against the second Bigfoot, which was crouched on top of him. "Help me," Stephen screamed as the Bigfoot snapped its teeth and slashed him with its claws cutting his arm. Stephen punched the beast in the face, which did little. "Henry, Victor," Stephen cried.

Victor stepped forward and hesitated as his eyes turned cold, stone like, blank voids. He watched as the Bigfoot's giant fists pummeled Stephen with all of its beastly might. Stephen fought back, but the monster's strength was too much.

"Help me," Stephen mumbled in confusion, his voice sounding weak.

A malicious smile touched Victor's face, his eyes turning hard with an inhuman vehemence. With a sneer, he raised his glock and unloaded it into the Bigfoot until it collapsed on top of Stephen. Victor took a deep breath and sighed with perverse contentment. He slowly walked over to Henry's still body and kneeled down.

"Dead," he whispered and smacked his lips with a perverted pleasure. He stood up and walked towards Stephen who was coughing and with one arm was trying to push the heavy weight of the Bigfoot off of him. His left arm was completely pinned. The night vision goggles were still on the side of his bloody face.

"Henry, Victor," Stephen called out weakly. "You guys okay?"

Victor stopped and watched the struggling Stephen with a sadistic amusement that emerged from within a dark place he had kept hidden most of his life. He felt powerful and in complete control, the same feeling he had experienced as a child, stepping on beetles, burning ants with a magnifying lens and smashing flies. When he was a teenager the need for control, to have another life completely in his hands, progressed beyond insects. He could no longer stop his urges and killed a cat with a bat. It was a neighbor's cat that had been around for years and was always walking through Victor's backyard. Victor never played baseball despite his father's insistence, but there was an aluminum bat in the garage. Victor always viewed the neighbor's cat as a nuisance, an intruder that had no place in his parent's backyard. He never liked pets. With little thought, as if a spell had been cast over him, Victor had taken the aluminum bat and beat the cat to death. He could still hear it screech. His parents had been away and no one ever found out. He put the bloodied corpse in a bag and dumped it in a garbage can two alleys away from his house. Killing the cat had given him much pleasure, but even more when he heard his neighbor calling for his lost pet. It had been the only time he had committed such an act, but the memory of that dark pleasure had remained with him into adulthood.

And now when opportunity arrived, while he stood there watching Stephen struggle in futility, the dark pleasure returned stronger and better then he could ever dream or remember. It was enticing him. Drool dripped down one side of Victor's mouth as he watched, his eyes growing more vicious. Stephen struggled just like the cat had done seconds before he had taken its life. He stepped towards Stephen and smiled. "I'm here Stephen," he said.

"Victor," Stephen called out. "Are you okay?"

Victor took another step closer until he stood over his boss, his cat from childhood. "More than you could ever imagine."

"Help me out from under here," Stephen rasped and trying to place his night vision goggles over his eyes with his free hand. Victor swooped down and ripped them off and threw them down the tunnel.

"What the hell? What are you doing?"

"What I was meant to do," Victor smirked, his cold eyes beaded. "Stephen it's time to take the company in a new direction under my direct control. You've been an obstacle since our companies merged. I would never have allowed it, but I needed the cash."

"Are you insane? Help me out of here. Where's Henry?"

"Henry's dead and now it's your turn... say a prayer Stephen." Victor kneeled down and with both his hands picked up a rock and raised it over his head. "You're my cat," Victor mumbled in a crazy fervor, his face blank of any human emotion. With a grunt he smashed it over Stephen's head. Stephen yelled and cried out. Victor raised the rock a second, a third and a fourth time smiling as he committed murder. When he was sure Stephen was dead Victor dropped the rock, stepped back and laughed insanely. He stood for a moment until some semblance of humanity returned to his cold demeanor. More plans began to churn in his perverted mind.

Victor glanced once more at Stephen before turning around and rushing up the tunnel towards the surface.

CHAPTER 21

Chad Gamin woke to the sound of a woman's blood curdling scream. His eyes were closed and his thoughts sluggish as he tried to comprehend what was happening. He was conscious enough to realize that he was resting on his back on cold, rocky ground. A piercing headache burrowed behind his brow straight to the center of his head like a nail, his entire body ached and felt numb and cold. He was unsure where he was or how he had gotten there or if all of this was just a bad dream.

The woman screamed again, louder and more frantic for her life, calling for help, jolting Chad a little closer to reality. "It's not a dream," he thought in a muddled daze. He started to slip back into unconsciousness when he forced himself to concentrate, latching onto the woman's screaming in the black muddle of his mind. With much effort he opened his eyes to darkness. He blinked several times and slowly the black turned to a dark gray as his eyes adjusted and focused.

"There must be a faint light source somewhere," he thought just as his eyes shot wide open when he heard the too familiar apish grunting of a Bigfoot. There were at least two of the monsters somewhere nearby. He gritted his teeth fighting back the growing terror and struggled to move his numb right arm. What seemed like an enormous amount of time passed as the woman screamed. Chad pulled his right hand free out from under a weight that was pinning him. Weak and trembling, his fingers found the hilt of Vengeance and gripped it. He pulled his knife out and felt slightly more secure.

He took several deep breaths and tried to sit up. The piercing pain that wracked his head brought a wave of dizziness. Chad swayed nearly falling back down. He turned towards the screaming and was surprised to see a man sleeping right next to him. He found that there were people lying across the entire floor of the cavern. There were a few flashlights scattered on the floor among the mass giving some light to the chamber. Near the far wall to his right, two Bigfoot were pulling a struggling woman across the floor towards the black entrance of an adjoining tunnel. The taller Bigfoot seized both of the lady's arms while the other one tried grabbing at her kicking legs.

Chad's vision began to spot with black dots as another wave of dizziness rushed over him. He dropped his head feeling nauseous and raised it again determined to help the lady. He lifted Vengeance and started to stand up when his vision faded to black as he passed out. Chad collapsed to the floor as the woman screamed.

When Chad woke up the cave was unnervingly quiet. He had the vague impression of a person lying next to him, but he was lost in a daze. He was not sure if the screaming woman had just been a nightmare. He needed to escape he realized as some clarity seeped slowly back into his mind. He turned his head to the right, the harsh pain lancing through his skull. He opened his eyes again and saw the dark shape of a sleeping man next to him. He reached over and touched his arm.

"Hey," Chad whispered. "Wake up." The man did not respond so Chad shook him firmly "Wake up," he said a little louder." The man remained motionless so Chad sat up despite the pain that throbbed behind his brow. He cringed as he found a morbid sight. The man was dead, his neck broken and twisted in an unnatural manner. Desperation and a sense of panic broke out on Chad's face as he looked at the other sleeping people realizing to his horror that they were all dead. There was a woman only ten feet away covered in blood and another woman with chunks of flesh missing from her stomach and the arms appeared to have been eaten off. Bodies were piled everywhere, some in stacks that were five feet high.

All the memories came rushing back as Chad examined his own body. His clothes were torn, blood soaked and he had scrapes and bruises all over. His left eye was swollen and the back of his head was caked with blood. His lower lip was split. What exactly had happened? He had just finished eating a sandwich at the sub shop in the general store when he heard the cry of a Sasquatch. And then the unbelievable occurred. The Sasquatch invaded Hyder? How? Why? Several of them had attacked the store. He had been with Mrs. Measly and her grandson. They fought valiantly but there were too many. The last thing Chad remembered was firing his gun as the Bigfoot charged his position.

"They must've dragged me here with all the other town folk," he thought and then the horrifying realization hit him. All these dead people were the citizens of Hyder. It made him sick to his stomach; so many dead, so many lives destroyed.

Chad searched for his glock and to his despair found it missing. He pulled out a handgun from his coat and thought, "This will have to do." About 15 feet away was a flashlight between two bodies. He started to stand up to retrieve it, but sat back down as the dizziness returned. His entire body felt exhausted, weak and sore.

His thoughts turned to Andrew and Alberto. Were they okay? Had they escaped the destruction? Were they alive? He glimpsed warily at some of the faces of the dead bodies near him praying that he did not see his friends. Andrew had stayed at the bar drinking a martini while Alberto had gone back to the inn. Was it possible that the Sasquatch had attacked the entire town? How many of the beasts were there? Why did they invade the town? Chad shivered as he thought of his father. If Andrew was correct, these were the same Bigfoot who killed his father. These were the same monsters that started this nightmare for him four years ago.

For five years Chad had been a struggling screenplay writer in Los Angeles when his life had been turned upside down and shattered the day he had decided to go camping with his father. He had experienced and survived encounters that no man had ever had to face. "I must be crazy," Chad thought. "Angry," he corrected. Memories of his father and more recently of Sherrie, Andrew's daughter, who had helped him escape the Ape Caves, reignited the ire inside. Sherrie had been killed minutes before help had arrived. It was unfair. Chad gripped Vengeance, the same knife that Sherrie had used to defend herself until the end.

Chad focused on Sherrie and his father, promising them he would survive. They would expect no less. The pain that drilled behind his brow continued undiminished. He began to stand up to grab the flashlight, but stopped when a deep deafening roar blasted through the cave coming from the adjoining tunnel where the Sasquatch had dragged the screaming woman earlier.

Chad quickly laid down on his back gripping Vengeance in one hand and the gun in the other. Heavy scrapping footsteps were heard in the distance getting louder and nearer until Chad knew for certain at least, one Bigfoot had entered the cavern. The footsteps stopped and the beast began sniffing as if it was trying to catch a scent. Chad remained still, trying to breathe as faint as possible so as not to attract any attention and to blend in the dead that surrounded him.

The sniffing continued for several seconds before the Bigfoot hacked and coughed for a long, unbearable moment. It cleared its throat and burst into clicking, apish grunts, excited as if it was celebrating its victory. Chad flinched slightly at the noise and squeezed the handle of Vengeance for security. He pondered if he should stand up and shoot the monster, but caution prevailed. Gunfire would surely bring many more of them rushing into the cave and with just a knife and a handgun, he would stand no chance. He decided to wait it out. Once the monster left, he would search for a way to escape and leave his chance to fate, luck, prayer and skill.

The grunting, clicking noise died down and then the footsteps began again, growing closer. Chad forced his hands to stop trembling from fright. He had faced these monsters before and the only way to survive was to keep a clear mind and not to give in to panic.

The footsteps made a loud slapping noise, as they kept getting nearer, until Chad was sure the beast was only a few feet away. The footsteps stopped and the only sound remaining was the monster's heavy, deep breathing and occasional cough. Chad could only imagine the Bigfoot standing above him scanning the corpses with its black eyes looking for any sign of life. He restrained the almost uncontrollable urge to open his eyes, raise his handgun and shoot before the monster attacked him.

"Be calm, Don't let it win." Images of Sherrie and his father seconds before they were both killed flashed through his mind.

The Bigfoot sniffed again sounding louder and right over him. Chad remained completely still. "Sherrie, Sherrie, Sherrie," he thought in repetition, her name giving him some sense of calm.

With a shocking fright, the corpse of the man next to him began to shake. Chad flinched involuntarily and went still, praying the beast did not detect his movement. The Bigfoot growled low and quiet, deep in its chest. Chad closed his eyes tighter, his teeth clenched.

"Sherrie, Sherrie, Sherrie," he repeated like a mantra fighting back the terrifying reality that he was alone in a cave with at least a dozen blood thirsty, murderous beasts. The corpse of the man jerked forward and was suddenly pulled over Chad's stomach and legs.

Chad nearly fired a shot by accident and removed his finger from the trigger. It seemed an eternity as the heavy weight of the corpse was dragged across him.

Finally the nightmare was over momentarily and all was silent until the Bigfoot ripped pieces of clothing off of the corpse and dropped them to the floor. Some of the shredded clothing fell on Chad. "What the hell was it doing?" Chad thought as part of him wanted to open his eyes to see, but he did not dare.

Chad soon found out the disgusting answer when the Bigfoot bit into the corpse tearing the flesh, making loud chewing and chomping sounds before it swallowed loudly. It was the most disgusting noise Chad had ever heard, his stomach churned with nausea.

The Bigfoot took another bite, chomping and swallowing quickly in a ravenous manner. It devoured the corpse in a frenzy. It took another bite and a bone snapped. Chad kept still, wishing this entire episode of hell would end. The Bigfoot coughed and spit up something, salvia splattering on Chad's face. He cringed and kept his hand still even though he wanted to wipe.

The feeding continued and Chad tried not to picture the scene, unable to get the thought that the beast was devouring a man in front of him, out of his head. Had he met this poor soul before in Hyder? The town was small and he was sure he must have passed him and everyone else who lived there many times on the street or at a restaurant. The townsfolk always waved and said hello or wished him a good morning or evening. It was a far different mentality than Los Angeles where people ignored each other. His hometown of Longview was more in line with Hyder on the courtesy level, especially when he walked along Lake Sacagawea where most said hello.

The chewing finally stopped as it walked away dragging the corpse behind it. The heavy footsteps grew fainter until the cavern became silent. Chad took a deep breath, sighed and wiped his face. "I have to get out of here," he thought desperately, keeping his eyes closed until he was sure the monster had left the cave.

After several minutes went by Chad opened his eyes and gasped. A dark, shadowy figure stood over him. It stepped nearer and in the dim, gray light the figure turned out to be human... female. The woman, tattered clothing hanging from her body, dirty face, long ratted hair that fell down past her shoulders, looked at him for a moment, her eyes growing wide with recognition.

"Chad," she said in a faint dry voice as if she had not spoken in a long time. She stepped closer. "Chad Gamin," she stated louder, her voice cracking. "It's me, Meredith."

CHAPTER 22

Victor emerged from the cave barreling into the thick undergrowth covering the entrance, batting his arms madly to break through, his face contorted with panic and a giddy satisfaction. He broke through the foliage reaching the clearing where he halted abruptly, his jaw dropping in shock. The helicopter, his escape, was overturned, the sides dented in and the propellers bent. With anxious eyes he scanned the clearing, raised his glock and rushed over to the helicopter. He found the control panel smashed.

Victor wiped the drool off his lip and reigned in his terror, his eyes growing hard and beading. Nothing would stop him now that he had crossed a forbidden line. He was now free from all human constraint and morality and he reveled in that fact. He fished out his cell phone from his jacket and dialed the second helicopter.

"Phil, it's me Victor. Come to these coordinates immediately. Do not pick up Andrew. I repeat do not pick up Andrew. Get your ass over here now or you're fired. Understood? Stephen's dead," Victor yelled into the phone, his pale face flushing red. "You can't talk to him or anyone else. Bill, Henry, all of them are dead. Now hurry up." Victor clicked the phone off and gazed at the tree line shaking his head in frustration. "There's going to be some big changes at the company," he muttered, his eyes tightening with a disturbing gleam while future plans began to churn in his wicked mind.

At the Stewart airport, Andrew's face creased into a sneer, his eyes bulging with frustration. "Pick us up. Victor told you not to? I don't care if he outranks me. We need the chopper. Chad's missing? What, you can't be serious. Stephen's dead? Henry and Bill too? For God's sake, pick us up. We need to help." Andrew hung up the phone and stuffed it in his pocket grumbling under his breath.

"What's going on?" Alberto asked.

"According to Victor, Stephen, Henry and Bill are dead. The second helicopter is going to retrieve Victor who gave the order not to pick us up. What the hell is going on?" Andrew stamped his cane on the ground.

"This is getting worse," Alberto said. "I can't believe everyone is dead."

Andrew stormed off cursing and yelled. "This is bullcrap. We need to find out what is going on and find our teammates." The thought of all of his comrades dead shook Andrew to the core. He had spent decades searching for the Sasquatch and never once had he lost a team member to these beasts until the Ape Cave Horror where everyone was killed including his daughter. The joy he thought he would experience discovering the Sasquatch had turned into a nightmare of regret, sadness and rage. His idyllic view of the creatures had been shattered. "If only." These two words appeared in his mind again. If only he had not been so stubborn and fool hardy and had equipped his team properly with firearms, something Chad had suggested, his daughter Sherrie, Enrique, Javier and Ted would most likely be alive.

"And now it's happening again," he thought in dismay. His new team of professional, armed men had been wiped out. Chad was missing and he did not dare think what might have happened to him. He felt responsible for Chad's safety since he had manipulated Chad into joining the expedition to Mount Saint Helens. Afterwards they shared a bond of surviving the Ape Caves. On some levels, Andrew saw Chad as the son he never had, who had spent the last minutes with his daughter before her horrific death. It had made Andrew a very happy man when Chad had agreed to join his team. It made the last year, with all the difficulties dealing with his daughter's death, more bearable.

"And what of Stephen?" Andrew thought. Was his friend and employer truly dead? Stephen had funded Andrew's operations for the last three years. The money had come at the right time since Andrew's fortune was gone. The last couple years before the massacre at Camp Elizabeth had been tight. No one believed in the Sasquatch and it had been difficult to find funding.

Besides the money, Stephen worked well behind the scenes, organizing, delegating and making Andrew's outfit into a world class, efficient operation. Without all this funding, Andrew would have been limited to driving around in a van.

"If Stephen was dead, then what would happen to the company and the Sasquatch operation? If everyone was dead did it really matter?" he thought with a morbid feeling settling upon him.

"I don't really care at this point. I have to find Chad." Andrew stamped his cane on the ground and noticed Alberto watching him, worried and scared.

"What are we going to do boss?" Alberto asked.

Andrew looked about the airport, which was bustling with activity as more police and medical teams arrived. A couple reporters had already landed a few minutes earlier, asking questions and getting into everyone's way.

'They'll be swarming this place like flies," Andrew thought. Alberto stared at him waiting for an answer. A determined scowl pressed into his haggard face. The lines creased as his temper flared. "We're going to get ourselves a damn chopper and find Chad. I have the coordinates to the cave that Stephen went into. We'll start there."

Alberto turned and followed Andrew. "I feel too damn old," Andrew thought. It was rare for him to feel old, always on the move, busy with projects, interviews, research; he rarely stopped. When he looked at his deeply creased, wrinkled face and white hair in the mirror he saw an old man, not the same image of himself that he had in his mind. He rarely felt old inside. He did not worry much about his looks like some people his age who spent a lot of money on plastic surgery. But today, he felt old and the weight of the night's attack began to burden him with exhaustion.

The image of Casey kept appearing in his mind. The little girl reminded him of Sherrie, who always played outside as a young child, so happy to see him when he returned from one of his treks. He had missed out on too much of his daughter's childhood, always away on his adventures searching for the Sasquatch. He never regretted missing birthdays, holidays and everyday life at the time, but now he was laden with guilt right in the center of his chest. His daughter was dead, gone forever. He could barely think the word, "dead." It was too horrible. Only in the last few years when Sherrie had joined his team, had they spent time together. "Thank God," he mumbled, but on the other hand, Sherrie was dead because she had joined his foolish quest. "I'm an idiot," he thought with regret as the anger began to boil and rise again.

"Chad, if you're out there. I will find you," Andrew promised and walked into the airport building.

112

CHAPTER 23

Chad looked up at the haggard woman looming above him in the shadows, who had called herself Meredith. Her wide, wild eyes stared back in astonishment as she knelt down beside him. The only Meredith that Chad had ever known died four years ago when a Bigfoot pulled her through the window never to be seen again. This woman next to him looked completely different. Where Meredith was overweight, with full, thick, black hair, a jolly expression, chubby cheeks, this person was gaunt, thin, grayish hair and sunken cheeks. This could not be Meredith. No one could have survived capture by the Bigfoot for four years. "They would have killed her a long time ago like they murder everyone else. "It's impossible," Chad thought. "No way in hell."

"Who are you?" Chad asked.

"Meredith," the woman whispered in a dry voice. "I can't believe it. You're alive Chad. Is it really you?"

"Meredith?" Chad examined the woman. Her pale, white skin was dry, creased and dirty. The woman offered her hand. Chad gripped it and found it cold and bony.

"Camp Elizabeth," the woman said in a horse voice. "We went to that cabin where that blond woman let us in, gave us dinner and called her husband. Help was coming, remember? I went to the kitchen and the next thing I remember is waking up while being carried by one of these monsters."

"Meredith Smith," Chad stated in unbelief. "You're alive!"

"You are too," she gasped with joy and gave him a tight hug, not letting go as tears streamed down her face. Chad hugged her back feeling slightly dizzy as he stood up, a pain still lancing inside his skull. Meredith felt like skin and bones as they hugged. She also stunk but he did not care.

"Oh Chad," Meredith said. "I just can't believe it. The good Lord answered my prayers. I prayed everyday that you made it, that you escaped and that blonde woman... Claire, wasn't it?"

"She died that night," Chad said. "I was the only one to escape."

Meredith sighed and squeezed him harder, mumbling, "I can't believe this... I thought I'd never see another person again and then I find you. How long has it been?"

"Four years." All the memories crashed back into Chad's mind of that fateful day when they were fleeing through the woods towards the lake hoping that someone was at the cabin to help.

"Four years," Meredith cried. "It seems like an eternity. I've been in so many caves; I've rarely seen the sun in all this time. It just seems like an endless nightmare," she rasped, her voice sounding drier as if speaking was too much for her vocal cords.

"How have you survived so long with these monsters?" Chad asked still flabbergasted that she was alive. "They kill everything they capture."

"Igor," Meredith muttered the name with disdain, her face screwing up with disgust. "Igor has been my blessing and my curse."

"Igor?" Chad pushed her back a little so he could look into her eyes.

Meredith chuckled. "Must sound stupid, but I'm a little crazy after all this time. The only thing that has truly kept me alive and going is the good Lord. Igor is one of those bear men, a Bigfoot or whatever those damn things are. It found a liking to me. It's a huge hairy beast, hunchbacked with a big lump on its back. The other bear men are scared of him. Igor has protected me from the others. It's done things to me Chad, things that no woman should ever have to go through."

"Oh Meredith." Chad gave her another hug. "I'm so sorry."

Meredith shook her head as if trying to dispel the bad thoughts. "Where are we anyway? We've been in so many different caves and we always travel at night. We've been in this tunnel longer than any other place."

"We're near Hyder, Alaska."

"Hyder?" Meredith's voice cracked. "That's over a hundred miles from Camp Elizabeth. What are you doing in Hyder?"

"I escaped that night, thinking you were dead. About three years later I joined a Bigfoot hunting outfit and we came up here because of some Bigfoot sightings. We've been in the area for the last few weeks. The Bigfoot attacked Hyder, knocked me out and I woke up here."

Meredith gazed at all the bodies that filled the cavern. "These must be the people of that town. I've never seen them take so many before. Usually it's a lone hiker, occasionally three or four people but nothing like this. I knew they were up to something evil. These demons have to be stopped."

"Meredith, if I had known you were still alive… there were so many search parties looking for survivors and the Bigfoot, but they vanished. No one found any trace of them."

"They're smart, devious sons of bitches," Meredith spat in disgust. "They're not dumb animals. They're intelligent and evil. What scares me even more is that their behavior has changed recently. They've been sitting with their leader chanting as if they were calling out to something, praying to some dark force. I don't know what, but I sure know they ain't calling out to God."

"Chanting?" Chad asked.

"It's the scariest sound I've ever heard, loud screeching and deep baritone humming, but there's a pattern to it."

"We'll talk about this later. We've got to get out of here, find a way to escape." Chad let go of Meredith and picked up the flashlight laying a few feet away next to a dead woman in her 30s.

"There's no escape Chad," Meredith rasped, her voice devoid of any hope. "I've tried many times. They won't let us go and they'll come after us in numbers. They'll kill you. Igor will probably keep me alive."

"We have to try. I'll do everything in my power to see that we escape." Chad flashed the handgun in the light. "Help will come eventually."

"No help, no one ever comes down here alive. No one knows we're down here. If they do the Bigfoot will disappear again. They always have an escape route. They will break up into small groups and meet weeks later in some other damn cave. They're freaking devious."

"Not this time." Chad clicked the gun. "I'm getting you out of here alive. You have a son to see again."

"How is Daniel?" Meredith asked her eyes welling over. "How is he? Have you seen him"?

"Only a couple times. He's happy, living in Portland."

Meredith bowed her head and cried. "He'll be fine," she murmured and looked up at Chad with wide, wild eyes. "I know why the good Lord has kept me alive for so long in this hell. Finally, I have an answer to my prayers."

"What?" Chad asked.

Meredith smiled reveling in her epiphany. "To save you."

At that moment a woman cried out somewhere in the cavern. "Help me," a muffled voice broke the quiet behind them.

Chad turned and flashed the light over the floor of bodies where across the room he saw an arm move. Chad rushed over, climbing over the corpses. Meredith followed, waddling slowly behind unable to put much pressure on her knees. Chad saw a hand waving out from under the corpse of a dead fat man. Chad pushed the body to the side and to his shock found Mrs. Measly on her back, her glasses cracked and her face bloody.

"Mrs. Measly," Chad gasped and helped her stand up.

"Chad," Mrs. Measly cried. "My arm." Her right arm was broken and hanging limply to her side. Chad helped her out from under the bodies and sat her down.

"You have to leave," Meredith said. "They'll be coming soon."

"My grandson," Mrs. Measly said. "Where is he? I can't see a damn thing without my glasses."

"We're all leaving tougher," Chad said pointedly at Meredith and began flashing the light over some of the other bodies nearby stopping on a familiar coat worn by one of his teammates. "Greg," Chad whispered and rushed over to find him dead. Chad opened Greg's backpack and found a 9 mm and two explosive devices. He tore off the flannel and quickly made a crude sling for Mrs. Measly's arm.

"My grandson?" Mrs. Measly kept repeating. "Where is he?"

"I don't know," Chad whispered. "Be quiet. We're leaving now."

Chad handed the 9 mm to Meredith. "Remember how to shoot one of these?"

Meredith smiled. "Remember... I ran Camp Elizabeth with Frank for years. I have known how to shoot a gun since my dad took me out in the woods as a kid. I even taught Frank how to shoot. I was the first one to take him hunting after we got married."

"I found these explosives too. They should come in handy."

"Show me how to use them," Meredith said as she clicked the safety off the 9 mm.

Chad looked at Meredith and both their eyes made contact. Chad saw a determined sternness and resolve in her eyes tempered with relief. The woman had to be damn strong to survive so long in Sasquatch hell. Behind the strength was a depth of sadness, but also peace. He glanced away a moment and showed her.

"Simple, set the timer and press this button to activate and then run. I've already added the verification codes."

Meredith took the explosives from Chad's hands and put them in a worn pocket in her tattered shirt. "You have to go now Chad and take Mrs. Measly with you."

"You're coming too Meredith. I just found you. We have so much to talk about. I want to see you safe… happy…to see your son again."

Meredith shook her head slowly, tears streaming down her face. "I can't go. The good Lord has kept me alive to save you and Mrs. Measly. I should be dead by now like all the others." Meredith pointed to the piles of bodies. "These demons have to be stopped and I'm the only one who can do it. By the time the police find this cave, they'll be long gone and will strike again and kill more people. I can't let that happen again. They are evil and bringing more evil to this world. Whatever they are chanting to, calling out to, in the black of the cave, it's real. I can feel its evil eyes looking at them getting closer every day. Whatever it is, it's worse than the Bigfoot. Maybe killing all these people was some sort of blood sacrifice to this power. I don't know, but these Bigfoot killed my Frank, killed Jay, killed your Father, my friends, hunters from Longview who had been coming to Camp Elizabeth for years. They are all dead now because of these demons and now they slaughtered an entire town. No More. This stops now. Lord Jesus kept me alive to save you and stop this evil. My prayers have been answered. Chad, this is the happiest day of my life. I'm so glad to have seen you one last time." Meredith pulled off her wedding ring. "Give this to my son and tell him I love him, tell him to go to church and pray to God. I will see him in heaven."

Chad took the ring.

Meredith hugged him and stepped away. "That goes for you too. Go to church and pray to Jesus. I will see you in heaven."

"I will," Chad said. "But you don't have to do this. Come with us."

Meredith shook her head with firm resolution. "I can barely walk. My knees were bad four years ago; you remember that. I would only slow you down. You'll have your hands full with Mrs. Measly. That's not my destiny. The Lord has another path I must travel. Go Chad before it's too late. You'll never know how good this day has been for me."

A monstrous roar thundered through the room causing all three of them to gasp and tremble at the furious sound. They all froze for a moment as the noise reverberated in their chests. Chad turned to look and on the other side of the room stood a massive Sasquath hunched over in the shadows with a bulging hump on its back. Its thick, wide body was bent in a deformed position, its clawed hands touching the ground.

"It's Igor," Meredith cried. "Go that way and follow the tunnel. It will take you to the surface. Go Chad. I love you."

"Love you," Chad said to Meredith then grabbed Mrs. Measly's hand and rushed across the room. Meredith watched them go for a few seconds as tears of sadnesnes, resignation and joy dropped from her eyes. She smiled and looked up. "Thank you Lord." After Chad and Mrs. Measly disappeared into the adjoining tunnel, Meredith stood tall and faced Igor.

CHAPTER 24

Igor rushed across the chamber leaping over the piles of bodies, jagged teeth flashing as it roared, charging for the tunnel that Chad and Mrs. Measly had just entered.

"Stop," Meredith rasped in the loudest voice her weak vocal cords could muster. "Stop Igor." The massive, deformed Bigfoot with a bulky growth on its back which looked like a giant tumor with patches of hair growing on it, came to a halt towering over the frail woman who could barely stand. Igor breathed hard and growled spit spraying out of its mouth as it stared down at Meredith with its bulging black eyes. It gazed at her for a moment and glanced at the far tunnel ready to begin pursuit again.

"Stop Igor," Meredith commanded and looked up at the beast with crazed, stern eyes and smiled. "Let them go. They are my friends. You've killed enough today." Igor's attention remained on the tunnel where Chad had fled and it started to take a step towards it.

"No," Meredith yelled and clasped the beast's hand. Igor frowned and grunted in displeasure and brimming anger. With a calm expression Meredith locked eyes with the beast that had been her protector, kidnapper and tormentor for the last four years. Igor stared at her and growled in a tempered tone; its dark eyes studying her. She released its hand and took a couple steps back. Igor watched as she raised the 9 mm. Meredith fired five times striking Igor in the chest, shoulder and stomach. Igor stumbled back and fell over gasping and choking on its own blood. Meredith walked over aimed at Igor's head and pulled the trigger. Igor made a wheezing sound and went still as Meredith stood over its body and laughed, something she had not done in years. The release felt so good to her and she wiped a tear from her eye.

"Goodbye Igor." She cackled in a surge of happiness before her face turned serious again. She kneeled down next to Igor's lifeless body and reached for its hand where on the very tip of its hairy-clawed pinky finger was a silver ring. She pulled the ring off and threw a vengeful glare at Igor as if the beast was still alive and rasped loudly, "That's Jay's ring. It was never yours." She put the ring on her finger and looked up at the black of the cave. "I'm sorry

Jay. I promised I would get this ring back and I did. I never should have given it to that demon."

Jay had been part of the thirty hunters who had gone on that fateful trip to Camp Elizabeth four long years ago. He had been one of the few survivors of the initial attack saving Meredith's life and hiding with her in the cellar of her cabin. They had journeyed through the woods with Chad trying to escape the Bigfoot that were relentlessly pursing them, heading for a lake where a stranger's cabin stood on its shores in hopes of finding help. Jay never made it. A gray, scarred Bigfoot had ambushed him right before they had reached their destination. Meredith killed the son of bitch that murdered Jay, shooting the monster several times as it tried to chase Chad up a tree.

After getting revenge, Meredith had returned to Jay's body and retrieved the expensive engagement ring he was planning on giving to his fiancé. Unfortunately, Meredith never made it back to civilization. The ring turned out to be a Godsend. The first time Meredith tried to escape, Igor had caught her almost immediately and looked like it was about to kill her until she offered Jay's ring. Igor surprisingly took it and tried to put it on its pinky finger. Meredith had found it morbidly amusing. For several nights Igor had caressed Meredith's wedding ring on her finger and now it wanted one of its own. Igor had worn Jay's ring ever since.

Meredith looked down at Igor one last time, her hatred gone. It had done so many horrible things to her, but now that was over and the beast had paid for it in death. The Lord had kept her alive for a reason and now she had the answer why. It made her happy to have a sense of purpose again and her prayers answered. "Only I can kill these demons," she called defiantly out into the darkness all around her. She stepped away from Igor's corpse and never looked back as she prepared for her destiny.

She picked up a flashlight, squinting, the illumination hurting her sensitive eyes. She had spent so much time in caves suffering in the pitch black and rarely saw daylight. The Bigfoot only traveled during the night under the cover of trees. Her one pleasure was to catch a glimpse of the stars through the branches and if she was lucky the moon, especially if it was full. She had never realized how bright the moon really was at night in the dark of the wilderness and away from the lights of civilization.

All the anger, pain, loneliness, sadness and terror she had lived with vanished as she went to her place of peace deep inside her soul and prayed to God for strength to do what she knew she had to do thanking him for letting her see Chad one last time. This place of peace she had withdrawn to countless times, almost disconnecting from her body, protecting her from the fear of being in the midst of murderous monsters. She wondered each night if this was the time they would turn on her. She always had nightmares of the Bigfoot devouring her alive.

When Igor molested her, Meredith would withdraw to her place of peace and pray to God, forgetting everything else. Whatever happened to her physically, the monsters would never be able to get to her refuge. She was free there and felt the presence of God protecting her. For most of her life she had never been much of a churchgoer. She and her husband Frank, who had been murdered by the Bigfoot at camp Elizabeth, liked to spend Sundays sleeping in, watching television and barbecuing. This ordeal had brought her much closer to God. It was the one good thing that had come out of her imprisonment. She had always wondered why God had kept her alive and now she knew.

Meredith opened her eyes and left her place of peace returning to the cold and black of the cave filled with bodies. "Give me strength God," She whispered and walked by the corpses of men, women and children. "I will get vengeance for all of us," she rasped taking quick glimpses of some of the dead faces, so lifeless and cold with looks of terror frozen on their faces. "For Frank, Jay, Claire…" Meredith whispered naming as many hunters from Camp Elizabeth that were killed that she could remember. "Thank you God that Chad survived. Help him and Mrs. Measly escape this hell."

Meredith limped slowly into the tunnel on the opposite side of the cavern from the one Chad and Mrs. Measly had entered to escape. Chad was heading for the surface while she was walking deeper into the bowels of the Bigfoot's lair. Meredith moved slowly, grimacing as her knees throbbed in pain threatening to give out. She had so little energy left, starved and unable to keep the raw meat down that the Sasquatch provided her. Occasionally she would eat berries, nuts and roots, but hunger constantly plagued her.

Meredith limped around a bend in the tunnel and found two Sasquatch females with their hairy breasts sagging over their fat bellies. They stared at her and hissed, raising their hands to protect them from the light that Meredith shined in their faces. "Get away," Meredith rasped. "You bitches." Out of all the Bigfoot, the females hated her the most, but left her alone fearful of Igor's wrath. She thought about shooting them and decided to save the bullets. The bitches would be dead soon enough. "All of you will die... you hear me?" She yelled and walked by them as they hissed at her and spit, some of it striking her face.

"To hell with it," Meredith cursed and aimed the 9 mm, unloading the gun until the Bigfoot bitches were dead. She hesitated a moment and started firing again, her face brimming with glee as she peppered their fat bodies with bullets. The gun clicked empty. Meredith laughed hard and deep and flung the gun at the head of the nearest bitch. With the flashlight in hand she hobbled down the tunnel.

Meredith had lived in so many caves during the past four years especially at the beginning when the monsters were fleeing after the massacre at Camp Elizabeth. The Bigfoot knew full well that many men would be after them so they were always on the move.

They had been living in this current cave for at least six months Meredith guessed. "Maybe a year," she thought having lost all concept of time in the endless days and nights in darkness. Once they had reached this cave, Meredith had immediately noticed a change in the Bigfoot, as if they had finally reached their destination. The Bigfoot had started gathering in one of the deep chambers and listened attentively to their leader, a mean, monstrous Sasquatch, grunt and click as if it was teaching them something. Shortly afterwards, the Sasquatch began to chant once a night praying to something or calling out to some nameless terror. It sent chills down Meredith's frail body even thinking about it. The chant was composed of high-pitched shrieks and screams followed by low grunting that would build into a loud monstrous roar. And then the Sasquatch would become silent all at once sitting in the darkness motionless like they were waiting for a response to their demonic prayer. The silence was scarier than the chant. Meredith would sit and listen in a nearby tunnel wondering what they were doing. She had never witnessed such behavior from them during the entire time she had been held captive. The silence lasted ten to twenty minutes until the leader grunted and broke up the gathering. The Sasquatch would return to their normal routine until the next assembly.

They chanted every night or day; Meredith had no idea of the time except that it occurred on a regular basis. Meredith's lips tightened as she gripped the flashlight tighter at the memory of the last time the Bigfoot had chanted. Whatever they had been praying to, finally answered. Meredith shuddered at the thought. The Bigfoot had gone through their chant followed by silence as usual. Meredith had been outside the chamber sitting exactly where Igor had placed her. The monster never wanted her to be far from its grasp. When the chant had finished, all the Bigfoot had become quiet and from the silence, something answered. The air pressure had changed slightly as if something of great magnitude had entered the chamber. Meredith had felt a presence, like a shadow falling upon her. She remembered that she had wanted to flee down the tunnel at that moment but she did not want to attract this intruder's attention, so she sat still in the dark and listened to the silence, alone and afraid. Meredith shook in fright at the memory of what had happened next.

A, low deep humming began at what she could only describe as waves of static electricity passing through her body making her hair stand on end. The humming was deep, growing louder and it was not coming from the Sasquatch. The sound vibrated the base of her skull and the center of her chest and Meredith wondered if it was sound at all or something else. Maybe the hum was some other form of communication being transmitted to her mind. The hum increased in intensity and then she heard a voice speak. She could not begin to comprehend what this presence had said, but she knew it was evil. Each syllable dripped with hatred, malice and venom. It spoke only for a brief moment. "A demon," Meredith had thought. Whatever the Sasquatch had been calling to was even more wicked than them. This demon was intelligent and Meredith had dropped down to the ground as close to the cave wall as she could hoping this power would not detect her. She could feel it look in her direction, but it continued to speak in deep tones in an incomprehensible language. Each word reverberated through her body. She trembled at such power and felt that if it found her, it would destroy her. She was sure its evil eye was getting closer when it stopped suddenly. The instant it spoke the last word, the humming and the wave of static electricity vanished as the air pressure returned to what it had been before this wicked encounter.

The devil spawned creature had withdrawn and Meredith immediately felt relieved. She began to breathe again not realizing that she had been holding her breath. She had never experienced such pure evil first hand and never wanted to again. Seconds later, the Sasquatch had erupted into high-pitched war cries and most of them left the cave to attack Hyder.

"A blood sacrifice… it had to be. That demon demanded blood," Meredith thought as she hobbled down the tunnel. The Bigfoot had brought back an entire town of bodies.

Without warning, a Bigfoot emerged from the darkness and stormed by her grunting in displeasure. Meredith gasped and quickly regained control of her fear.

"God has kept me alive so I can wipe out this evil and stop this demon from coming through to earth," she whispered wiping a joyful tear from her eye. "Thank you God, thank you. I knew you did not forget about me. I will stop them and in doing so I will free myself of this dark hell."

Meredith reached the entrance to the chamber where the leader resided and where the Bigfoot came to chant every night. She set the timers to each explosive device for ten seconds. She took a deep breath and whispered, "You better be in heaven Frank. I'm going to be pissed if you didn't make it." She thought back on that fateful day when the nightmare had started. She had been cooking hamburgers for Frank, her husband of 22 years, when the bear men had attacked Camp Elizabeth. One of the monsters had knocked down the cabin door and in seconds killed Frank right in front of her. Meredith gritted her teeth banishing the memories.

All the pain will be gone shortly. "Be strong, be strong, be strong" she thought as stepped into the chamber of the leader and flashed her light.

Over twenty Bigfoot turned in her direction all at once, grunting and growling in warning, some shielding their eyes from the brightness. Many of the Bigfoot were sitting on the floor while the others were standing in groups. The leader stood at the other end towering above most of the other Sasquatch. Big, muscular and frightening, the leader glared at her with the blackest eyes.

Meredith shuddered as all of her enemies stared at her. She fought back the urge to turn and flee. "Lord Jesus," she rasped quietly and walked slowly into the chamber towards the leader, weaving in and out of the Sasquatch sitting on the floor. As she neared one of the Bigfoot, the beast growled and swiped at her signaling her to leave. Meredith was under Igor's protection, but she was intruding into the inner sanctum and did not know how much longer she had until one struck her.

Meredith had never been so bold, always staying close to Igor. She knew that they all hated her and could see the confused expressions twisted on their faces. They were baffled at her intrusion wanting to attack her, but did not because she was Igor's property. This advantage of surprise would not last long so Meredith limped as fast as she could through the room.

These evil beasts had killed too many people and she would stop them this very day. They would hurt no one else and whatever this dark, evil force they had been calling to, Meredith was going to make damn sure that it was never contacted again.

Meredith approached the leader with bold steps. The leader stood up to its full height and looked down at her flashing its teeth and snarled. Meredith dropped the flashlight to her feet, took the two explosive devices in both of her hands and pressed the buttons.

"Go to hell," She rasped and raised the explosives above her head and smiled, her eyes beaming with happiness, relief and peace. The leader roared and extended its clawed hand to strike, but it was too late. The bombs exploded annihilating everything in the cavern in a cleansing, white heat.

CHAPTER 25

Chad led Mrs. Measly through the tunnel, which twisted and turned giving them no idea what was waiting for them up ahead. He held the flashlight in one hand and the handgun in the other. The tunnel was narrow with rock walls protruding out. Chad fought back the desire to turn back and take Meredith with them whether she liked it or not. He already felt guilty for leaving her although it had been Meredith's choice. It still seemed hard to believe that she had been alive this whole time. He could not imagine what she had had to endure and experience during the last four years. Chad's experiences with the Bigfoot had been pale in comparison. Meredith had been their prisoner. "She's one strong lady," Chad thought. He had tried to convince her to return to the surface with him, but she refused mentioning something about God's plan, the Bigfoot chanting to something and wiping out their evil. "I hope you succeed Meredith," Chad thought. He hurried as fast as he could with Mrs. Measly crying out, her broken arm being jarred in the makeshift cast.

"My grandson Chad," Mrs. Measly said. "We have to find him."

"We'll find him, but first we have to get out of here and call the police."

"Everyone's dead... all those bodies. It's the end of the world. They destroyed Hyder... those damn monsters... My store... I've been running it for the past 11 years since my husband died."

"Be quiet," Chad snapped. "We have to be quiet."

"Yes, yes," Mrs. Measly mumbled.

They turned a corner and Chad halted spotting the dark silhouette of a body up ahead. "A Bigfoot," he whispered, approaching it cautiously. He aimed the gun and stepped closer.

"Is it dead?" Mrs. Measly whispered.

Chad flashed the light over a puddle of blood around the beast. "Looks dead," Chad whispered, leading Mrs. Measly around the corpse, as far away from it as he could, along the cave wall. "There's more," Chad gasped. On the other side of a boulder, in the middle of the cave, were five bodies, some of them looking human. Chad approached slowly and found the bodies of Stephen, Henry and Bill as well as two more Bigfoot. Chad kneeled down next to

Stephen and grimaced. Stephen's face was covered in blood, swollen, as if it had been smashed by a heavy object. He checked for pulses on all three bodies and found no sign of life.

"Who are they?" Mrs. Measly asked.

"My friends... that one over there is Stephen Denmin, the man who funded and ran the organization I worked for."

Mrs. Measly nodded. "He came into the store many times, a very nice, gentleman. I'm sorry Chad."

"Thanks... but this does not look good."

They moved past the bodies avoiding the hairy corpses of the Bigfoot and continued up the tunnel. Chad felt numb emotionally and seeing the bodies of his teammates did not affect him at the moment. He had seen so much death and destruction caused by Bigfoot he almost came to expect it. He was leaving Meredith who had survived all this time, who had saved his life four years ago, who was saving his life right now, behind to fend for herself against all the Bigfoot. He felt like a coward, but she had remained behind for him, for herself and for everyone that these monsters had killed.

They turned another corner and up ahead stood a rusty ladder. Chad gripped the cold metal and shook it. "Seems sturdy enough. We're going to have to climb the ladder. Do you think you can do it?"

"I'm old, I have a broken arm, but I ain't dead. I've outlived my husband, most of my relatives, shot a bear, not to mention that my father always said I was built like a brickhouse. If that's the way up, to escape, I can damn well do it."

Chad smiled. "You go first. I'll be right behind you."

Mrs. Measly gripped the ladder with her good hand and stepped up the first rung. "I could use a little help."

Chad put the gun in his pocket and pushed Mrs. Measly, step by step, up the rusty ladder, creaking under their weight. Mrs. Measly cried out once when she bumped her broken arm on a rung. Chad kept looking back down hoping not to see a Bigfoot rushing towards them with claws out-stretched.

Mrs. Measly reached the top and Chad followed. He pulled out the gun and shined the light down a slightly larger, square tunnel with half buried rails down the middle. The air did not smell as foul on this level.

"Fresher air," Chad mused.

"How long is this god-forsaken tunnel?" Mrs. Measly hissed.

"Too long, but I think we're getting closer to the entrance."

They rushed down the tunnel, turned a corner and stopped abruptly. Ten feet ahead stood a Bigfoot startled by their appearance, obviously not expecting them. It was near eight feet tall with a thick build. The surprise lasted only a second before its face creased with rage as it charged. With no hesitation Chad blasted away with the handgun firing several shots before the beast dropped knocking them to the ground as it fell. The beast snapped its teeth and slapped at them sluggishly. Mrs. Measly kicked at it and Chad scooted back firing his gun several more times until he was sure it was dead.

"That's what you get you son of a bitch," Mrs. Measly yelled. Chad helped her stand up and then maneuvered around the dead Sasquatch. They soon reached a mound of dirt blocking the tunnel, which looked as if the entire ceiling had collapsed.

"Oh know! We're trapped," Mrs. Measly muttered.

Chad rushed forward to one side of the dirt mound finding it completely blocking the tunnel. Had they taken the wrong tunnel? Were they trapped? Chad felt the panic begin to rise. He shined the light along the top of the mound hoping to see a way through the blockade. He finally reached the other side and came across a narrow opening. "Looks like it goes all the way through. Come on, I'll help you."

They climbed over the uneven ground of the rubble. Mrs. Measly had trouble with her broken arm and Chad had to help pull her through. The dirt was loose and they both slipped as they moved through the narrow opening. Chad's head ached and his bruised and exhausted body felt weak. He gritted his teeth and managed to get Mrs. Measly over the mound. The air immediately grew fresher on the other side.

A few minutes later they saw light up ahead. Both of them hurried even faster, anxious to reach the surface. Chad glanced back thankful that they were not being pursued. They exited the cave and pushed through the dense undergrowth finding themselves in a clearing surrounded by trees. A helicopter was on its side, bashed, bent and demolished.

"Looks like our helicopter," Chad remarked. Suddenly the ground shook and a muffled explosion boomed from within the cave. Rock began to crack and the whole cave collapsed sending boulders falling from the cliff face as a puff of dirt and dust shot out. Chad and Mrs. Measly ran into the clearing as rocks rolled past them. Chad looked back and said, "Meredith." She had accomplished her mission and had died for the second time.

They rushed past the helicopter and moved into the woods spotting a lake in the valley below.

"Do you know where we are?" Chad asked.

"I think that's Briar's Lake several miles north of Hyder."

"Briar's Lake," Chad pulled out his cell phone, surprised to find that it still worked and called Andrew Bridgeton.

CHAPTER 26

The Scout kneeled down and felt the faint vibrations in the ground and heard the rumble of an explosion. It looked with wide eyes and spotted a dust cloud filling he sky in the direction of its cave. It growled deeply, stood up and rushed through the forest leaving caution behind. Something had happened to its home. It raced with panic and rage creasing its hairy face.

The Scout reached the entrance to the cave minutes later and found it buried in rubble. The entire side of the hill had collapsed concealing the cave completely. It rushed over and began lifting up boulders and heaving them through the air trying desperately to dig its way in as it roared in furious rage.

A short time later the Scout stopped and growled in futility, frustration growing evident on its hairy face. Its home had been destroyed and most of its brothers were probably dead. It raised its head to the sky and roared loudly, the sound echoing through the valley with blistering ire. It picked up a rock and flung it at the manthing's flying bird that it had destroyed earlier. It walked into the clearing wanting to lash out, destroy whoever had done this, but no one was near. It sniffed and caught a fresh scent, a familiar scent; one it had not smelled for a long time. It dropped to the ground sniffing the scent trying to remember where it had smelled it before. A look of recognition dawned on the Scout's face. The scent belonged to the young male manthing that had escaped several seasons ago. The Scout and its brothers had wiped out the manthing's camp and pursued the few survivors through the woods to a lake. One manthing had escaped on a boat into the lake. The Scout and some of the others had swam out to kill the last living manthing, but at the last minute, the flying metal bird rescued their prey and flew him away.

The scent was fresh, meaning the manthing was near. The Scout slashed at a tree sending chunks of bark shooting through the air. This young male manthing was the cause of the destruction of its home. The Scout would kill the manthing and it would not escape this time. The Scout rushed into the woods after Chad Gamin.

Meanwhile, up on a nearby plateau Victor yelled, "What the hell is going on?" A plume of dust rose up from where the mine entrance had been seconds after he had felt tremors shake the entire hill. He had two men with him and a new helicopter resting on the rise overlooking the valley. He had commanded the pilot to land on a nearby hill, close to the mine for a look out location. The Bigfoot were in the mine below and he planned to wait until he spotted one emerge to the surface. The radio was filled with reporters, police, and military. They had little time to find one before the whole area would be swarming with people. Victor wanted a live specimen to experiment on and test some ideas he had been thinking about for the last few years. Suddenly, the whole side of the hill had collapsed in a thunderous roar.

"Had a bomb gone off?" Victor thought, wondering what had happened. His plans had just been destroyed in front of his eyes. The entrance to the cave was buried under tons of rock and debris. How could any of the Bigfoot survive? Who the hell let off a bomb? Time was running out and he was growing angrier by the minute.

"What should we do?" one of his men asked with a distraught look on his face after hearing about the deaths of Stephen and the others.

"Stay here and keep your eyes open, both of you. Use the binoculars. I want one alive." Victor would wait and hope one of the beasts had survived.

"They killed Stephen. We should kill them," The pilot snapped angrily.

"Alive," Victor yelled as thoughts of shooting the pilot flashed through his mind. He pushed back the enticing thought. He had to control his urges no matter how much pleasure he had gotten from killing Stephen.

They sat on the plateau waiting and a short while later the pilot cried out, "I see something, movement near the base of the cliff, by that rock outcropping."

Victor looked into the telescopic sights of his rifle and saw a dark, hairy shape crawling out from under the dirt-covered rocks. "It's a Bigfoot," Victor said. "Must've found a way out. Looks hurt. Take a shot, put it to sleep."

The pilot fired the tranquilizer rifle and missed. The Bigfoot looked up in their direction and crawled faster towards the cover of the trees. The pilot shot, a dart striking its back. All three of them rushed to the helicopter and a few minutes later they found a place below to land. They spotted the Sasquatch, adolescent, nearly six feet tall, unconscious near the trunk of a tree. It was covered in dirt and had several abrasions on its body.

"Tie it up and put it in the chopper. No one must know about this. Keep this completely confidential. Don't tell your girlfriend, your whore, your drinking buddy, no one… understood," Victor snarled.

Both of them nodded.

"Understood," the pilot said and pointed to the beast. "It's bleeding. Looks pretty beat up. It stinks too."

"Let's just get the hell out of here," the other man said nervously. "There might be more around here."

They quietly packed the Sasquatch in the helicopter and flew off. Victor looked out the window with a sick, smug smile on his face… all of his plans were coming together.

CHAPTER 27

Chad and Mrs. Measly had just reached the shores of Briar's Lake when a high-pitched, shrill roar broke the quiet of the woods somewhere close behind them. They both froze for a moment, coming to a standstill at the ferocity of the sound, which echoed through the valley. Mrs. Measly gasped and nearly fell down with fright. Chad, who had been on the phone the entire time giving Andrew directions and discussing what had happened said, "Hurry Andrew, We're being followed and I don't have a gun."

"We'll be there in minutes. Hold on Chad," Andrew said.

"Hurry," Chad cried and clicked the phone off. He put it in his pocket and withdrew Vengeance from its sheath. He grabbed Mrs. Measly and led her to the edge of the choppy waters as far from the line of trees as possible. The sun was high in the sky and a cold wind blew, white clouds dotting the blue of the day were moving quickly. The ground was covered in icy snow that made it slippery to walk. Branches snapped and leaves crunched, as something moved through the undergrowth towards them. Chad let go of Mrs. Measly's hand and raised Vengeance. Mrs. Measly kneeled down and picked up a rock with her good hand. Chad grimaced, breathing hard as he scanned the trees. Andrew had found another helicopter that was used for tourists to go sight seeing and had paid the owner for the use of it. He was on his way.

"They won't get here in time, will they?" Mrs. Measly whispered.

"They will," Chad assured her, his eyes never wavering from the perimeter in front of him. He knew the Sasquatch were fast, clever and any lapse of concentration could be deadly. Chad took a deep breath as the headache in the back of his skull flared harder. He felt sore and weak, but luckily adrenaline was keeping him going.

Another roar thundered loudly, reverberating deep in their bones, sounding much closer than before. Chad shuddered, as it seemed to last forever, fading to an uncomfortable silence. Only their heavy, quick breathing could be heard, faint and weak compared to the war cry of a Sasquatch. Chad knew it was close by watching them. "I hope there's only one," he thought. They would have no chance if there were more. Without firearms they would be hard pressed to survive an encounter with just one of these monsters.

The silence continued for another two minutes and then a branch snapped as a rock the size of a television hurtled through the air, whooshing over their heads and smashing into the lake a few feet behind them sending a spray of water splashing against their backsides. Mrs. Measly yelled in a terrifying gasp and tripped falling to the ground Chad jumped forward in surprise and nearly lost hold of Vengeance, but recovered quickly.

A Sasquatch over seven feet tall, mean and muscular, its face twisted in boiling rage, burst from the tree line and in a blur charged down the bank towards them. Chad fought back the desire to flee, kept a steady hand, raised Vengeance over his head and threw the knife with all of his might. Vengeance sliced through the air, the blade glistening in the sunlight, sticking deep in the Scout's stomach. The Scout howled angrily, clenched its teeth and came to a stumbling halt. It pulled Vengeance from its gut and dropped the bloody knife to the ground. Dots of red spotted the white snow around the Sasquatch as blood sprayed from the wound, matting the hair on its stomach. The Scout held its gut with one hand and growled, taking a step towards Chad who moved to the right away from Mrs. Measly who was still on the ground desperately trying to stand up with her broken hand slipping on the slick, icy rocks.

"Hey," Chad yelled, waving his arms.

The Scout turned towards Chad, snapped its teeth and rushed forward, its eyes brimming with fury. It would kill this manthing no matter what. It would not let this weak, small thing escape a second time. The manthing had destroyed its home and now it would end his pathetic life.

Chad fled down the uneven shores of Briar's lake, sliding over fallen logs, barreling through bushes, splashing through a shallow creek that tumbled over a rocky bed. The Scout charged after him, knocking through any obstacle in its way, slowed down by the knife wound, the blood dripping between its fingers.

Chad climbed a dirt bank that crumbled under his weight sending him falling into the foot deep water of the creek. He jumped up and scrambled over the bank as the Scout gained on him. Gasping for air, his body sore and exhausted, he pushed himself even faster. He reached a fallen tree four feet in height blocking his path and instead of slowing; he pushed off the top with two hands and leaped over it. The Bigfoot circled around giving Chad an extra couple steps in distance.

All of a sudden, Chad pushed through the branches of a tall bush and the ground dropped out from under him sending him tumbling down a slope into a muddy gully where standing water, covered in a thin layer of ice, cracked upon impact. The water was cold and shallow. Chad stood up covered in mud and dripping with icy water. The Scout reached the top of the gully and glared down at him with beaded black eyes. It jumped and crashed down to where Chad had been standing a second earlier.

Chad lunged out of the monster's grasping, clawed hands and climbed up the side of the gully, clutching exposed roots to pull himself up. The Scout rushed after him, but slipped and fell to its knees. It lunged with one arm out-stretched tearing into the slope inches below Chad's foot. It growled, pushed itself up and climbed up after him.

Chad reached the top of the gully and stumbled slamming his knee hard against a rock. He gritted his teeth and climbed over the bank. The Scout was close behind him. He grabbed a rock the size of a football and lifted it over his head as the Scout snarled from the brush. Chad hurled the stone and sent it pounding against the Scout's shoulder. The Sasquatch continued forward, unfazed, as it held its stomach, blood squirting heavily through its fingers.

The Scout reached the top and rushed after Chad, who broke through the brush and found himself back on the banks of Briar's Lake. Mrs. Measly was nowhere in sight and he had no place to run. The Scout reached the rocky shore blocking his way. Chad backed up to the edge of the water that lapped quietly behind him as the Scout pressed forward. He had little room to run to the left or the right. Either way would put him in reach of the monster's long arms. The Scout growled; its eyes seemed to beam with satisfaction knowing that it had trapped its prey.

And then out of nowhere, a helicopter appeared buzzing loudly over the treetops, circling low over the lake's water. The door of the helicopter opened and Andrew Bridgeston leaned out aiming a rifle and fired. The gunfire boomed and the Sasquatch stumbled back as blood spurted out of its chest. It gasped and collapsed, falling on its back with a big hole near its heart. It struggled desperately to get up, spitting up large amounts of blood. It fell back down gasping for air as it choked on its own blood. It turned its head and glared at Chad with violent rage and tried to slash at him with its arm, but the movement was slow and sluggish. Its arm dropped to its side and its breathing became shallower as its eyes dialated. Chad backed away from Sasquatch moving a few feet to the right along the water that lapped against the rocky bank. The Scout became motionless seconds later and its eyes stared lifelessly up at the blue sky.

Andrew waved at Chad who gave him the thumbs up. Chad turned back and gazed at the Sasquatch that lay only a few feet away. He approached it cautiously until he was standing over it. This beast had tried to kill him and who knew how many people it had murdered. He stood there exhausted, breathing hard, covered in dirt with pieces of leaves and shrubs hanging from his clothing. His face and body was bruised and bleeding from fresh scratches. He looked at the Sasquatch with disdain. There was a bloody hole in its chest from the bullet and an open wound from Vengeance. Even now when it was dead, the sight sent chills through his body. It was scary standing so close to a creature of such great power and death. Chad felt no pity for the beast and stepped back away as images of it seizing his leg with one of its giant, hairy hands flashed through his mind. He did not ever want to be this close to one of these monsters again whether it was dead or alive.

Chad caught movement to his right as something burst through the undergrowth. He stumbled back in surprise and sighed when he saw Mrs. Measly emerge from behind a tree brandishing Vengeance, the blade still bloody, in her good hand.

"Chad," Mrs. Measly called out. "Are you okay?"

Chad nodded. "It's dead."

Mrs. Measly limped over and glared at the Sasaquatch. "I thought that damn thing got you. If I had a gun I would have shot the bastard myself. It's dead and burning in hell. We need to find my Grandson."

Chad nodded. "Andrew will fly us back and we will report this location to the police. They will be all over this place soon." He doubted her Grandson was alive and was most likely dead, buried under tons of rock in the mine. He thought of Meredith again, who was now truly dead. She had sacrificed her life to destroy the entire clan of Sasquatch. "She's in a better place now," Chad thought and waved for Andrew to land. He gave Mrs. Measly a hug.

"Thanks for saving me," she said.

Chad nodded as they walked slowly towards the helicopter where it had landed in an open area down the shore of Briar's Lake.

CHAPTER 28

Two months later at a Mexican restaurant in Longview, Washington, Chad took a bite of his chicken taco, leaned back and asked, "So what's the big news you wanted to tell me?"

Andrew frowned across the table with an angry scowl creasing his pale skin, his gray eyes livid, blood shot and tired. He gripped the silver head of his cane, tapping it rapidly on the floor, a bad sign since he usually leaned it on the table or the chair while dining. Andrew took a long, deep breath and shook his head mumbling something as he smacked his lips a couple times. He exhaled slowly and locked eyes with Chad. "First off, the board of directors nominated Victor as president and CEO to carry on the work that Stephen had dedicated his life to. As you know, most of the board members were part of Victor's company before the acquisition so you know where their loyalties lie. It was also known that Stephen's wishes were for Victor to take over if something ever happened to him."

Chad nodded. "That was no secret or surprise. I knew this was going to happen."

"Yes, yes," Andrew hissed, his entire face screwing up with frustration. "But let me tell you the surprising news. I got a call today from Victor. He fired us. Can you believe that? He said we were no longer needed. All the equipment, vehicles, bank account that the company gave us, he's taking back. So we are effectively out of jobs and funding."

"What a dick," Chad said. "I never liked that slimy bastard anyways."

"He's an ass," Andrew quipped. "So the question now is what do we do next? That mineshaft is buried, collapsed under tons of rock and dirt. They'll never dig down deep enough to find their lair, which is most likely destroyed anyways. Meredith did what she told you she was going to do... bless her soul. I never knew her but I admire that woman. I never thought I would say it but I'm glad they're dead, the whole damn community of Sasquatch. Those animals killed my daughter. Meredith got justice for all of us. I wish I could have spoken with her. She lived with those creatures for four, long years. Just think how much she knew, how much she learned about them that we will never know. And then all that talk of chanting together in the cold, black of the cave... some sort of perverse prayer. Do you think she was crazy?"

Chad shook his head. "She wasn't crazy... She was obviously scarred deeply... anyone would be after four years, but I think she was telling the truth. I really don't know what to make of it? She kept telling me those beasts were evil and I believe her."

Andrew huffed, took a gulp of his beer and leaned back in the chair shaking his head. "There is the corpse of the Sasquatch I shot at Briar's lake to study. I have endless interviews to give, a book to write, documentary to film, but I want to know what you want to do? Do you still want to hunt the Sasquatch?"

Chad took a sip of his margarita, leaned back in his chair and shrugged his shoulders. He glanced out the window at the rain that bombarded the parking lot in sheets from the dark, gray sky. The cold wind gusted and people ran to and from their cars. "I don't know. I nearly died again. Meredith saved me from the cave and you saved me at the lake. I really don't know what I want to do next. I feel like my luck is running out. Most people don't survive their first encounter with the Sasquatch. This is number three for me. I got beat up pretty bad and still have headaches from the knock I took on the back of my head. What I really want to do is take a vacation."

"A vacation," Andrew murmured, "I don't remember the last time I took a vacation. My ex wife said my whole life was a damn vacation tramping through the woods."

"Want to go with me? I'm thinking about going to Puerto Vallarta. The beach is suppose to be fantastic, the water warm like bath water and the hotels are inexpensive. It will be sunny and hot. I need a break from the cold weather."

"Puerto Vallarta," Andrew mused. "Sounds like a good idea. I could use a vacation; enjoy some warm weather for a change. We could stay a few days in LA if you want?"

Chad shook his head. "No, no, no. No LA. I lived there for five years and I'm done with that place. I don't want to go back. I don't mind stopping at LAX for a layover, but that's it. My life in LA seems so long ago. I was a different person back then, pre-Bigfoot... I mean pre-Sasquatch, unaware that such monsters existed, unaware that they would kill my father and many others I cared for."

"Sherrie," Andrew muttered, dropping his eyes.

"Sherrie too," Chad nodded. "These beasts have taken so much from us. Did I ever tell you a couple of my pet peeves with LA?"

Andrew shook his head. "I don't believe so."

Chad took a drink of his margarita, set it down and frowned. "Well, first off, whenever someone asked me where I'm from, I couldn't just say 'Washington,' because they would always say, every single time, 'Washington, DC,' so I would have to say, 'no, Washington State,' so I started saying 'Washington State' right off. And my other pet peeve was I couldn't say 'pop' because everyone in LA says 'soda.' If I said 'pop' they would give me strange looks like I was some type of hick."

Andrew raised his hands in protest. "Okay, okay, we'll skip LA and just go to Puerto Vallarta." He placed his cane against the table, a sign that he was starting to relax.

"Puerto Vallarta it is." Chad smiled. "The good thing is we'll be at least a 1,000 miles from the nearest Sasquatch."

"You never know." Andrew shrugged his shoulders taking a long drink of his beer.

AUTHOR'S NOTE

You have survived the FURY. Congratulations!!!

The bad news is that you still have to face the Grandfather. He's mean, cranky and is out for vengeance. If you're not careful, the Grandfather might make you its next victim.

As you know by now, "Fury of the Sasquatch" is about the Bigfoot that survived and vanished at the end of "The Unleashing." It seems that in many of these types of stories, the monster disappears at the end of the book never to be heard from again. I always wanted to find out what happened next and unfortunately you never find out. So in "Fury of the Sasquatch" you and the entire town of Hyder got to learn what these secretive creatures have been up to hidden away in their deep caves.

In "The Grandfather," you are about to discover what happened to the handful of Sasquatch that survived "The Ape Cave Horror."

Please heed this warning: Don't stick your foot into any holes, especially if you think you hear coughing.

THE GRANDFATHER

In a hole in the ground near Mount Saint Helens, deep in the forest, something started to cough violently. Although a rotting tree trunk that had fallen over the year before concealed the hole, if one happened to be walking by, the wracking, intense cough could be heard. It continued in harsh bursts, wet, loud and painful sounding. Birds and other animals seemed to avoid the area as if sensing some sort of danger or threat. Only a few black ants crawling on the rotten log were oblivious to whatever lurked in the hole.

The coughing stopped and that area of the forest grew quiet, as if the trees themselves were sighing in relief, praying that whatever lived in the hole stayed in the hole. Minutes of peaceful quiet passed until a robin fluttered down and bravely perched on one of the overhanging branches, chirping in blissful happiness as the sun shined in the bright blue sky.

The robin squawked in fright, shot up in the air, its wings beating madly when the coughing erupted in a sudden fitful surge. Flying away, up into the brightness of the sky, the robin searched for another tree to rest on far from that disturbing sound.

While deep in the dark, dank hole, the Grandfather, an elder Sasquatch, hacked violently and spit up blood that splattered on the cold, dirt ground. It felt like its lungs were being ripped from its chest. Hunched over in the cramped quarters, it sat against the muddy wall and grimaced angrily at its condition.

The Grandfather's hand reached down to touch the thick, pinkish scar across its stomach. White, thin hair covered most of its body except for several bald patches that had grown larger over the years. Wrinkly skin sagged over its emaciated body, its bones, especially its ribs cage, protruding, making it look like a near skeleton. The Grandfather chomped its yellow teeth and growled as it touched the scar. Its stomach always ached and many times it was unable to keep food down.

The Grandfather's growls intensified, growing louder as the other three Sasquatch shifted nervously in the dark. The Grandfather's black eyes narrowed and it began to tremble with a building ire. They had lived quietly since its earliest memories, until the manthings came and destroyed everything. The manthings had invaded their home, killing many and forcing them to flee. Now they lived in a hole, going days without food. The manthings were everywhere, walking through the woods searching for them. The Grandfather heard the manthings flying machines in the sky above, day and night. The manthings had gone too far this time and the Grandfather was determined to strike back.

The Grandfather roared weakly and hacked up more blood. It had lost everything dear to it in a short time. Its eldest son, the leader of their family, the Father, had been killed as well as the Mother. Their bodies were buried in another hole nearby. It all started a couple seasons past when the deer, their main food source, grew sick, foaming at the mouth and turning violent.

The sickness had spread to some of its own kind and they had to be killed. The sick deer died off and were slaughtered by the manthings. They grew hungry, starving for days, having to forage longer to find something to eat.

And then the manthings discovered their home. The Grandfather traced the scar on its stomach with its gnarled finger as it remembered the old manthing with the light that had stabbed it. The Grandfather wanted to find that particular manthing and tear him limb from limb.

The Grandfather wondered about its youngest son. Before the manthings had invaded their home, the Grandfather had sent it to the great canyon in search of food. Its youngest son had never returned. There were only four of them left. Two of the young ones had gotten sick recently foaming at the mouth and died. Had the sickness that infected the deer returned? If the remaining deer got sick again then they would have little chance of survival.

The future did not concern the Grandfather, only the present. Revenge filled its mind. The manthings had attacked and now it would do the same. Grunting and clicking at the others, the Grandfather had been forced to take up the leadership again. It roared one last time, exhausted and leaned its head back against the dirt wall and fell asleep.

Hours later the Grandfather woke up. It sat a moment staring into the darkness as it rubbed its aching stomach. Pushing back the thoughts of hunger, the Grandfather growled low with a vicious edge until the others woke. The Grandfather had been hearing the voice again in its head, the strange voice that it did not understand at first, but as the nights had passed it began to comprehend. The voice was commanding it to find some type of object that was hidden nearby, something very old and dangerous. The voice had plagued the Grandfather's son, the Father, before the attack of their home by the manthings. Now that the Father was dead, the voice began to harass the Grandfather. It ignored the voice and focused on the task at hand.

The Grandfather crawled down the tunnel and the other Sasquatch followed. It stood up and touched the rotting log that blocked the entrance. It waited several minutes in silence and listened. When it was sure there were no sign of the manthings the Grandfather pushed the tree to the side with a loud grunt. It still had strength and rage to dispense. Its hand lurched from the hole and clawed at the forest floor. With a heave it pulled itself up and when it got to its feet, it glowered at the stars in the night sky. The other three Sasquatch climbed out and the Grandfather led them into the trees.

They moved quietly down a slope following a deer trail. The grandfather sniffed taking in several scents, all of them hours old. Its sagging frame seemed to liven with anticipation. Its eyes beaded with pent up fury. It would have its revenge that night. Up ahead a brook about two feet wide flowed down a slope. The sound of the water brought some peace to the Grandfather. It had always enjoyed listening to streams and waterfalls.

This time it was different for this particular brook signaled danger. One of the manthing's black boxes hung in the tree nearby. The Grandfather had spotted it a few nights past. It had been hiding in the midst of a bush waiting to scare a deer towards a younger Sasquatch crouched down behind a rock outcropping. The deer walked by the tree and the black box flashed. The Grandfather did not comprehend how the device worked, but it knew that somehow it would alert the manthings to their presence. Ever since their home had been invaded these black boxes were popping up everywhere hanging in many trees. One time the Grandfather turned and saw one of the contraptions staring right back at it, only a few feet away. The Grandfather smashed the box and flung it into the undergrowth.

The black boxes angered the Grandfather even more and it walked faster circling around the brook. In the distance one of the manthings vehicles rumbled and a dog barked. The Grandfather snapped its teeth in excitement. They were getting close.

They soon reached a clearing and up ahead was a manthing's house. Smoke bellowed from the chimney and bright lights lit the windows. The Sasquatch advanced towards the house.

Deanna placed a bag of popcorn in the microwave and grabbed a cola from the fridge. She pulled opened a cupboard and took out a bag of chocolates. Popcorn, pop and chocolate were a nightly ritual. She was in her mid-twenties, wearing sweats and a baggy t-shirt. She was overweight, had been her whole life. She liked to eat; eating made her feel good, especially in the evenings. Popcorn, pop and chocolate while watching television was her way of relaxing and brought temporary contentment.

The microwave buzzed and she took out the hot bag of popcorn and walked to the living room where her older sister Rachel, who had just turned 30, sat on the black leather couch, flipping channels madly.

Rachel frowned and sneered, "You eat that crap every night." She shook her head in disgust and continued changing the channels.

"I know." Deanna plopped herself on the recliner chair. "I have no self control."

"At least you started taking walks in the morning, but eating all that crap won't help, especially at night before you go to bed."

"Its comfort food," Deanna stuffed a handful of popcorn and a piece of chocolate in her mouth chewing with delight. The sensation of salt and sweet was so delicious. She smacked her lips. "It's the only thing that makes me feel good."

"How are you suppose to get a man if you don't lose weight?" Rachel asked without looking at her as she continued flipping channels.

Deanna stuffed her mouth with more popcorn and chocolates and shrugged her shoulders. Rachel had always been the pretty, skinny sister and she had always been the homely, fat ugly sister. Rachel had dated all through high school and college while Deanna did not even go to the high school prom. "Well how about you?" Deanna countered. "When are you going to get married? Settle down? You always told me that you wished you could fast forward your life to the point where you had your degree, a job, a husband and kids. You have a degree and you're a teacher, but no man?"

"There's George." Rachel offered and turned down the volume signaling that she wanted to talk. They had fought all their lives but since their parents had been killed almost three years ago, they had grown much closer.

Deanna took a big gulp of her pop. "George is a loser. He works three or four months out of the year in a cannery in Alaska making loads of money and then he spends the rest of the year in the bar spending it. You can do a lot better."

Rachel crinkled her nose. "There's not much of a selection in Cougar. The town is damn small."

Deanna nodded and took another sip of her pop. When the deer virus hit nearly three years before, Cougar had been dead center of it with a lot of people killed including her parents. Once the virus had been controlled and the rabid deer population annihilated, many residents of Cougar moved to other towns. And then if that wasn't enough, a year ago Bigfoot appeared out of nowhere and killed several people near Mount Saint Helens in what became known as the Ape Cave Horror. The attack occurred only about a fifteen-minute drive from their home and that caused even more people to leave saying that this town was cursed. The only benefit to Cougar was that the motels, stores and restaurants were always filled with scientists, tourists and Bigfoot hunters.

Deanna still found it hard to believe that Bigfoot had been living nearby in the forest for all these years. She had never believed that the creatures existed, even though she had grown up in the middle of Bigfoot country where sightings had been common. She always thought that they were hoaxes, caused by practical jokesters and publicity seekers. Deanna looked at her sister, took a sip of pop and said, "You need to move to a bigger town where there's a better selection of men. Vancouver, Portland, even Longview."

"My job's here… our home is here."

Deanna shook her head. "You can find a new job, not that I'm one to talk since I work at the convenience store. And this house was our parents' home. We're going to have to move on sometime. Too many memories linger in this place, plus we can sell it, we both need the money."

"I don't want to sell it," Rachel said. "We grew up here."

Deanna stuffed her mouth with another handful of popcorn and chocolate. She did not really want to sell it either. They had both moved back in after their parents' death and it had become a sort of refuge. Although she did see that they both had to get on with their lives and moving would help the process along.

"I don't want to…" Deanna stopped mid-sentence and looked towards the kitchen. Something had triggered the back yard light to turn on.

""Maybe it's a deer," Rachel said, unconcerned.

"Maybe." Deanna set her bag of popcorn on the light stand and struggled to her feet, out of the recliner. She had just gotten comfortable and was enjoying the conversation with her sister, but she knew full well she would not be able to sleep tonight if she did not investigate. Ever since that crazy deer virus, she habitually checked every window and door to make sure they were locked and only then could she go to sleep. Sometimes she checked three or four times a day. Her sister on the other hand was more careless leaving the front door unlocked which infuriated Deanna and was the cause of many arguments.

Deanna stepped into the kitchen, the linoleum floor creaking as she moved. Rachel remained sitting on the couch watching her sister. She turned the mute button on the television so all was silent except for Deanna's footsteps.

Stopping by the kitchen sink, Deanna peered out the window. The light illuminated most of the back yard except for the far end, which was covered in darkness. There was no sign of a deer or anything else. Deanna moved her head closer to the glass, her eyes squinting trying to look at the very back of the yard.

"See anything?" Rachel called from the living room.

Deanna walked to the backdoor and unlocked the deadbolt. "No… I'm going to look outside." Deanna opened the door, the hinges screeching from rust. As she stepped onto the porch she glanced around at the muddy lawn, the grass long. "Time for a mow," she thought and looked at the wooden fence standing six feet in height and lining the entire backyard. She was not sure, but it looked like the back gate might be open. Deanna frowned, not one to be spooked, she just had to make sure that the gate was shut and locked so she could have peace of mind. She stepped down from the porch and walked across the yard into the shadows. Her steps make loud splotching noises in the muddy yard. She found the fence gate standing wide opened and on the other side was a black wall of trees that led into the forest. The branches swayed in the wind making creaking and rustling sounds. A shudder shot through her body. Who opened the gate? Did Rachel leave it open? Her faced flushed red with a rising anger.

Deanna swung the gate shut and gasped. The bolt to the gate had been knocked off, the wood splintered and cracked. She glanced about unable to see much this far from the light on the porch. Her courage diminished giving way to fear. She rushed back towards the house spooked. Something was not right. She lumbered up the porch and into the kitchen, locking the back door. She rushed into the living room leaving tracks of mud along the way.

"It's busted," Deana cried frantically. "Someone busted the back gate. The bolt was loose and knocked off."

"Just now?" Rachel stood up her eyes wide with panic.

"I don't know. I didn't notice the gate opened earlier today. I've been home the entire day."

Something coughed, loud and wet. Deanna twirled around and looked towards her bedroom.

"Did you hear that?" Rachel said standing near the couch, her eyes growing wide.

Deanna walked to the bedroom and the coughing started again this time harder and louder. She entered the dark room and froze. A shadowy face was looking at her through the window. She gasped with a start, her eyes bulging with terror. The face drew nearer to the glass and Deanna realized in horror that it was covered in long white hair. Its nose touched the glass and black eyes glared at her. At first Deanna thought it was a man with a shaggy beard and hair, but she soon realized it was something worse.

Whatever was staring at her through the window opened its mouth revealing jagged teeth and it growled in a faint, dry voice. It raised its head and made a screeching scream in short bursts.

"What is it?" Rachel yelled from the living room.

The voice of her sister seemed to break the fearful spell of paralysis that had descended upon Deanna, who twirled around to run when the window shattered and a clawed hand reached in swiping at her. A monstrous roar boomed from the front of the house followed by high-pitch shrieks that sounded like they were coming from hell itself. The monstrous chorus was coming from every direction.

"Call the police," Deanna yelled, slamming her bedroom door shut. Rachel glanced about hysterically looking for her cell phone when heavy footsteps pounded on the roof, which creaked under something's massive weight.

"It's on the house," Deanna said.

Rachel had just picked up the cell phone when the living room window exploded inwards sending shards of glass peppering the carpet as something huge landed with a thunderous crack and stood up tangled in the drapes. Rachel dropped to the floor screaming and the behemoth ripped off the curtains and roared, thunderous and loud, standing over seven feet tall, thick and hairy. It looked down at Rachel who backed up against the couch screaming. It zoomed in on her with black eyes and flashed its sharp teeth taking a step towards her, the floor thumping loudly and creaking as it moved.

Deanna had no time to be scared. All she knew was that her sister was in danger. "Rachel," she yelled. "Run." She grabbed a book, the closest object within her reach, and flung it at the monster. The book bounded off its chest and had no effect. The Bigfoot roared and in one quick movement, reached down and seized Rachel's leg and swung her whole body through the air in a circle before smashing her against the wall. She hit with such impact that the wall cracked and made a hole. Bones broke and Rachel slumped lifeless to the floor. The Bigfoot turned to Deanna and snapped its teeth, its black eyes narrowing in on her, its next victim.

Deanna turned and ran into the kitchen her mind not quite registering what had happened to her sister. Her only thought was of escape. She opened the back door and rushed out onto the porch where the Sasquatch covered in white hair, the one that had looked at her through the window, stood, arms out-stretched, blocking her way.

Deanna lowered her head, raised her shoulder and barreled into the Grandfather, knocking them both down the steps to the muddy lawn. All in a tangle, Deanna yelled and pushed the stinking body of the Grandfather off of her and started to crawl away. The Grandfather grabbed her ankle and pulled forcefully. Deanna fell flat on her stomach in the wet, muddy grass.

"Get off of me," she screamed and kicked the Grandfather in the head with the heel of her shoe, but the beast still held on with one hand. Deanna kicked it again right in the face. The Grandfather slashed with its free hand striking the grass next to her. Frantically Deanna kicked both of her legs in a futile attempt to break loose, but the beast held on, its claws cutting through her sweats and into her skin.

Roars of the other Bigfoot filled the night sky all around. Deanna glanced back at the house in shock. The Bigfoot that had attacked them in the living room emerged from the backdoor holding the limp body of her sister.

Deanna yelled, her eyes flaring with anger. Instead of trying to escape. She scooted closer and kicked with all her might smashing the Grandfather in the head again and again. The Grandfather burst into a loud bout of hacking as Deanna struggled madly and finally broke free. She struggled to her feet and ran for the back gate. The Grandfather did not pursue her, remaining on the ground, its head bowed, coughing up blood.

Deanna ran. She had to get help. She had to call the police. She had to help her sister. As she reached the gate, she caught movement to her right an instant before a dark shape slammed her to the ground.

A third Bigfoot, shorter than the others, jumped on top of her grunting excitedly like some freakish ape as it slashed and hacked with its claws. Deanna fought back not feeling the deep cuts across her face, arms and chest. Her only thought was to help her sister as darkness took her.

The Grandfather struggled to its feet still hacking up blood. It touched its bruised and bloody face, glared at the fat female manthing that had done this and roared, a weak raspy sound. It signaled for the others to follow. Three Bigfoot appeared and walked over to the Grandfather, two of them carrying the female manthings that they had just killed. Despite the pain that wracked its body, the Grandfather was pleased. They would feast well that night. They had finally struck back at the manthings and now there would be two less of their enemy to harass them.

The Grandfather led the others out the back gate and into the woods. In the distance sirens could be heard and the shouts of other manthings. The Grandfather hurried its pace. They soon reached the hole. The Grandfather watched as the other Bigfoot climbed down into the hole with their prey. What looked like some kind of wicked smiled appeared on the Grandfather's face. It would be patient and hide for the time being, well aware that the manthings would be out in numbers after this attack. It would wait and when the time was right it would attack them again. Breaking into a hoarse, gasping laughter, the Grandfather climbed down into the hole, pulled the rotten log over the entrance and disappeared into its lair, ready to eat.

68351381R00083

Made in the USA
Columbia, SC
06 August 2019